THE ECHO

MORE SHORT STORIES
FROM THE LANDING

BY
MIKE R HUNTER

Cover photos and layout: Mike R Hunter
West Bay, NS B0E 3K0, Canada
Back cover pub: Reddit open source

ISBN 978-1-7780695-2-9 (print)
978-1-7780695-3-6 (e-pub)

A copy of this book has been deposited with Library and Archives Canada Legal Deposit.

http://mike-r-hunter.blogspot.ca

The Echo: More Short Stories From The Landing

The Echo

Table of Contents

FOREWORD

This modest collection of short fiction completes a project that was a happy accident.

After years of working on other people's book projects as Editor-in-Chief at Cape Breton University Press (Sydney, NS), I began a full-length novel of my own, a project that so far has had nothing but false starts.

As a way to get comfortable with writing dialogue, something I hadn't done a lot of – among other things never confessed – I started writing a few short stories and entered them in a few competitions in order to build some creative muscle. Near-total failure in that regard (writing contests, that is) did nothing to bolster my confidence. But a funny thing happened in the meantime. Characters kind of took over my imagination, becoming the focus and thus sidelining the novel.

The larger body of work that is "Stories From The Landing" was divided into two collections: one strictly humour, titled *No Place Like Home*, and this one, *The Echo*, consisting of stories that started lightheartedly but lean more toward the serious. It just seemed that there was a dichotomy of tone that could be best resolved by separating these from the outright humorous.

The title story of this collection, "Mac Talla – The Echo," speaks to the passion that people feel toward Cape Breton Island, its people and places, its communities, cultures, their history and histrionics and, of course, the music traditions. *Mac talla* is Scots Gaelic. It more or less translates as "the echo": that was the name of a Gaelic newspaper published in Sydney, Cape Breton, in the late 19th century.

These stories are works of fiction, triggered either by a real event or historical personage, or some little thing overheard in community settings, from which my imagination took over.

Depictions of the history, the buildings, geography and the people at the west end of Bras d'Or Lake where we live have been altered to suit the ideas behind the stories and may not reflect the reality. Many of the places and geographic references are indeed real, but here and there they've been "moved" to benefit the tale.

As with *No Place Like Home*, some stories are inspired by real people and events but developed in an unreal way. Some characters are composite (the same applies to places and histories), where I have blended this or that characteristic with someone or something else. Some stories do use the real names of real but deceased people or defunct institutions; I intend no offence to anyone. Such references may annoy anyone trying to read reality into a story or because they want to recognize someone. Where warranted, a few stories have been annotated at the end of the book for readers' further information.

Overall, the stories are meant to entertain, not teach or preach. You can go to bed satisfied with having read a good yarn, without lying awake pondering some unresolved dilemma or wondering what happened next. The beauty of short fiction is that not every story has to have a beginning, middle or (heaven forbid) a happy or tragic conclusion. Sure, someone else's story may have triggered the idea, but this is original fiction.

Now, about self publishing. These stories are of little interest to conventional publishers so, with apologies to former colleagues in the industry, I have gone ahead and done this myself. I'm not getting any younger and the stories have been rattling around in never-ending draft form for far too long.

Enjoy!

MRH

MADDIE'S GIFTS

"**A**ny messages?"

"Not for you," was the throaty reply. "Not today."

As she often did, Maddie occupied the old bench at The Landing, a rustic lichen-crusted seat a few metres from the rickety and seldom-used jetty.

A century ago, The Landing was a busy pier and jumping-off place for the long-since departed and never to return lake ferry. The bench was once for waiting; now it's just for watching. It's a quiet spot, mostly frequented by the herons, eagles and kingfishers that call a nearby tributary home.

There, Maddie sometimes waited.

Once or twice a day a passing car will pause and lower a passenger window to record the view on a mobile phone. Occasionally, the back of Maddie's once-ginger head was in the photo. At once visible and invisible, she paid them little mind while waiting for her ship to come in or her phone to ring.

It was beside her on the bench. Not a fancy touchscreen mobile phone like the tourists', but a dial-telephone like you hardly see anymore. It wasn't plugged in, of course. Like the non-existent ferry, it didn't connect anyone to anywhere. Nonetheless, Maddie waited.

One of those local characters just on the unnerving side of eccentric, Maddie lived in a ramshackle home at the edge of the village, the humblest of homes in the humblest of villages. You couldn't call it a house, for it leaned and probably leaked, was battered, though not broken, and weakened by neglect and poor management, though not yet defeated.

Rags hung for curtains in mismatched windows, the side door was propped shut by a mop handle. Never a light inside or out. A window in the barn sports a picture of a camel, of all things, and below that, a picture of a little lamb curled up in comfort, pictures from a nature calendar or magazine. On a breezy day, summer or winter, Maddie's unmentionables were shamelessly draped over shrubs around her overgrown front yard. There was no need for any "Keep Out" signs; passers-by instinctively quickened their pace.

Over the years, we never heard Maddie referred to by any other name, a cruel play on "mad," we supposed. To our shame, we knew little of her story, and what we did know, we learned from the opinions of others.

Not every day, but many, Maddie spent time in the village, pausing here and there for conversation, but keeping such encounters to a minimum. Now and then, she would stop and speak with no one in particular, laugh at some unspoken joke, berate some unseen tormentor, praise the largeness of the day, curse the cold and damp, or rant incomprehensively outside the village church.

∞∞

The weather was getting much colder, and Maddie slowly shrank from it beneath increasing layers of her third-hand winter clothing. Christmas was coming, and Maddie's place was decked out as always. She never failed to decorate her property according to the seasons and holidays. By All Saints Day, she carefully displayed pumpkins and a bale of hay in a nod to the fairies and goblins of Samhain in the Highland tradition. The day after Hallowe'en, is when she donned the first of her worn-out winter coats.

In December, a tangled string of Christmas lights – visible only in daylight – traced strings where, in summer, green beans had climbed beneath the overhanging branches of an ancient Caledonia pine.

"Beautiful day Maddie," I called, less to engage with her than to avoid startling her as we passed on our daily walk past the cove.

"Nineteen fifty blue," she nodded.

"Nineteen fifty?"

"The sky. 1950 blue. Like the song."

"Not blue like that anymore," I agreed.

"Your eyes are getting dim," she countered. "Like my memory."

"Any messages?" I asked, gesturing toward her phone.

"Not for you," was her throaty reply. "Not today."

After a moment she said, "he's coming this year," absentmindedly adding, "maybe Christmas."

"Your son?" my wife chimed. "How wonderful. How long has it been?"

"When's Christmas this year? The 25th?" she said suddenly, cackling at her little joke.

"What are you getting me this year?" I called. My wife gasped at my boldness.

"Same as last year." Maddie played along in that melodic Gaelic-influenced lilt so prevalent throughout the county, despite the fact that it hasn't been spoken for years hereabouts. "Same as next year," she added.

"He doesn't understand me anyway," she lamented. "Left me to rot in this shit-hole. Off saving the world, living the good life."

"You must be happy for him," I offered.

"Maybe this year, if he calls," my wife suggested.

Like many aging locals without children at home, we have downgraded our own holiday expectations. They're not off saving the world, and come only for measured visits.

There are hardly any youngsters around here, just us older folks, satisfied to share The Landing with each other in simultaneously increasing and decreasing numbers. We moved here in retirement a few years ago, purchasing a house abandoned by one of the foreigners who occasionally buy up land around the loch, only to leave again after a few years of failing to fit in.

I wondered how a child viewed Maddie. Does a son love and honour his mother no matter what? No matter his being "off saving the world," and her living in a shit-hole?

Neighbours say Maddie's mother disappeared under mysterious circumstances, but they add little else to the story. Maddie's father was a drinker, they say. One spring, he fell drunk off his tractor one last time. The tractor rolled right over him and kept right on going.

Maddie's younger brother followed, overworked and tired of the insularity of their tiny farm. Locals give a disapproving nod – as though in parentheses – when they mention that brother. The eldest brother never returned from the war. No one had any real understanding of the pedigree of the son Maddie sometimes mentioned or who, they wondered in whispers, was the father.

Alone, humiliated, proud and bewildered, Maddie withdrew. No one can say if she was truly mad, but there are stories like hers all around here, or so local lore would have it. Immigrant Scots, proud and feisty, broke their backs or went out of their minds making a better life for their families and descendants in this valley, only to see their sons lured to the good life on the mainland or killed in the wars.

I suppose it is we who make it difficult to engage with Maddie. Small talk is small. Even in retirement, our days seemed too full to risk getting caught up in a conversation we would not know how to end gracefully.

∞∞

That day, I ignored my wife's urging to keep moving and tried harder.

"What're you working on?"

Maddie's hands were always fidgeting as though worrying an unseen rosary. Today I could see that she was not just fidgeting but sightlessly engaged with an arrangement of long grasses that overflowed the frayed straw handbag at her side.

"Grandmother taught me," she held out an unfinished braid trailing fronds of beach grass.

"Oh my, it's wonderful." My wife reached out, but the object was quickly withdrawn.

" 'Snothin'," Maddie demurred.

∞∞

"Any messages?" We hadn't seen her for a week or more but on this day, Maddie was in her place, hands uncharacteristically still under a threadbare lap rug tucked in around her legs against the cold air.

"He's coming. He called me," she said quietly.

"He called you? Your son?" I'm sure both my wife and I instinctively glanced at the phone; I'm not sure we concealed our disbelief. By default, we doubted all but the most mundane of Maddie's remarks.

"Coming to get me. Take me out of this shit-hole."

"To get you?" I was dumbstruck. No small talk would save us from Maddie today.

Beside her on the bench, next to the phone, her straw handbag exposed a gift-wrapped box. A Christmas present, perhaps. Was she waiting for him here? Or for the non-existent ferry?

"For Christmas?" asked my wife. Maybe her son had invited her to his place. I was never entirely convinced that Maddie even had a son. Now I wondered if she really was mad.

"For you." Her palm, now out from under the rug, extended a braided Celtic cross held out as though for us to take. My wife hesitated, so I gently took the treasure from Maddie's hand, which was quickly withdrawn.

In perfect proportion, still warm from her grasp, the grasses were tightly and finely formed. Even the ring circling the intersection of the trunk and arms appeared as though stamped from a single sheet of yellow-green plastic.

I'd seen examples of the craft in books from the Hebrides, where people so gifted would craft practical articles – ropes, bridles and even buckets – from beach grass. Many people in The Landing are descended from the Isle of Lewis and no doubt plied the same ingenuity in times of spare resources.

"This is beautiful! So professional!" I motioned to return it, not wishing to presume that it was for us.

"Yours, I told ya." She smiled a sort-of smile and directed her eyes back to the loch.

"I'm speechless. It's beautiful. Are you sure?"

She shifted slightly in her seat and cackled, "don't say I never gave you nothin'."

∞∞

As much as anything or anyone around this end of the Bras d'Or, Maddie was, for us, an unspoken part of the area's charm. Like her ancestors now departed, she was part of the background, the back story, both known and unknown, seen but not heard, here but forgotten, visible and invisible.

It was not unusual for Maddie to be invisible for a week or two at a time, but we hadn't seen her for a little longer. We began walking a little slower if we passed her home, wondering between us if she was okay and hoping that she might see us and show herself – rather ironic considering our usual practice of hoping she wouldn't.

It was almost Christmas. With Maddie's Celtic cross now displayed incongruously in our secular home, my wife had the idea that we ought to give a gift in return. She chose a natural wreath decorated with silver-painted pine cones and a bright red ribbon purchased at a craft fair in town. We ramped up our courage and tramped up the icy path to Maddie's spiritless home before our daily walk.

The front door gave way under my knock, revealing that snow had invaded the entryway as though the door had been ajar for a time. There was no reply to our hollered hello, and, reluctant to breach the trust threshold just yet, we decided to see if perhaps she was out back.

We picked our way carefully through the snow-covered chaos of Maddie's side yard, lest we disturb anything, and rounded the corner of her back garden to be greeted by a private, crowded but tidy scene. In contrast with the chaos of the front yard, the back was orderly and ornate. Braided grass dolls perched in trees. Braided flowers 'grew' from broken pots and window boxes. Braided garlands were strung from tree to tree to tree. Braided crosses of every variant – Celtic, Christian, saltire – leant an air of devotion. This is where Maddie bided her time between visits to The Landing. This was her inside world, the Maddie no one saw.

"I have a bad feeling about this," I understated, worried that something had happened to her. My wife was worried that something might happen to us.

Puffing up our courage once more, we knocked this time on the side door. The mop handle that secured it fell immediately to the side, and the door swung outward as if relieved to be free. Inside, we entered a kitchen frozen in still life – a pot on the cold stove, a few dishes arranged neatly on the counter next to the sink, and a chair pushed back from the table. Calling for her again, though not expecting a reply, we followed our voices into the parlour – which was windowless in the old style.

What light there was from adjoining rooms illuminated the requisite painting of Christ and one of the Nativity, the star of Bethlehem faded by age and cynicism. Across the room stood a naked pine tree strung with garlands of her braided grasses. Beneath it were a number of gift-wrapped boxes of different shapes and sizes – at least twenty, maybe more – none very large, and all in various stages of yellowing from age.

Maddie's phone was on a small table next to a plain wooden bench worn to a shine from use. I couldn't resist picking up the receiver, half-hoping for a dial tone to contradict the cold emptiness of the house. But I knew it would be dead.

Across the room, my wife put down the wreath we'd brought, and retrieved two of the gifts. Brushing off dried needles, we examined the brittle gift cards. In the dim light we could see that more, perhaps all of them, had similar but nearly illegible inscriptions, as though she'd tried to erase them.

'To: Joseph, From: Màiri,' read one. 'To: [smudged] From: Màiri,' read the other.

"Màiri," I said quietly. "Her name is Màiri. Not Maddie. Traditional. Just sounds like Maddie."

∞∞

Two benches wait at The Landing, one engraved with a Celtic cross. Every Samhain, my wife and I decorate the Scotch pine growing between those benches with dollar-store bulbs, tinsel and garland, at once as charming and gaudy as Maddie's forgotten tree. Maybe she'd appreciate it, maybe not.

If we're around when someone asks, we tell them the bench and the tree are Màiri's.

"Màiri is a Gaelic name," we tell them. "There used to be a lot of that around here."

fin

THE NEW GIRL

"**D**o you serve lots of the liver?" he asked. One can't be too careful, you know.

"Yes dear. It's one of our favourites." Maggie MacPhail was sincere. It was the second-best seller on The Miller's Oven menu – second only to fish and chips, which is what I was savouring at the next table. Miller's home-cut fries are to die for.

"I'm not interested in *your* favourites," the customer said disdainfully. "Rather, in your *clients'* favourites." The English accent delivering that cutting remark doesn't impress in these parts, much less the attitude. London proper, I suspect.

"Right then," he continued, "liver and onions. Well-done, mind you."

"Mashed or fries?" Maggie asked mechanically.

"Mashed."

"Gravy?"

"I expect there will be plenty with the liver?"

"Anything to drink?"

"Diet Coke."

"Pepsi, okay?" Maggie turned her attention more cheerily to the woman across the table. "And for you, dear?"

"She'll have a tuna sandwich, white bread, butter not margarine, and a small salad, no dressing."

Maggie continued to direct her attention toward the woman, order pad and stubby pencil poised and ready. "Anything to drink, dear?"

"She'll have water, no ice. And weak tea with milk," he answered for her again.

"Save some room for pie, hons. Seumas there is known for his pies." Maggie gestured with a subtle lift of her chin to point out the kitchen, where a heavyset, ginger-haired cook was visible on the far side of the chest-high counter separating him from the servers.

The woman stole a glance at the glass doors of the dessert fridge next to that counter.

"We'll see," the Englishman muttered.

"Table six," Maggie called over the counter. "Tuna sandwich for the lady, liver and onions for his lordship."

The cook, Seumas, looked up at Maggie for a split second; a fleeting look passed between them before he turned his attention to the string of clothes-pinned orders descending in turn toward their eventual fulfillment.

Seumas was the only male staffer in sight. An air of masculine competence hung over his side of the counter. On the public side, four women, all on the grey side of middle age, moved gracefully and confidently among the tables – anticipating, asking and acting in the best interest of diners.

The Miller's Oven is unique, so far as I know, a long-time fixture of The Landing. Underwritten by two generations of MacKays, the diner had actually closed a decade ago when the local population had declined to an unprofitable level.

Not long ago, in part because of its long history and in part because its closure had left a hole in the social life of the community, a group of senior citizens – effectively the only remaining residents in the area –

acquired the place for a dollar and began operating it as a kind of co-operative. All pensioners, except the cook, they worked for tips rather than wages. Revenues went toward costs and operations. If they could, at the end of the year, dividends were donated to local charities. I stop in for lunch about once a month.

It is quite normal to see middle-aged-to-elderly women working as waitresses and cashiers – and not just here. It is also quite normal to see more women than men in a rural setting like The Landing. You don't necessarily notice it in larger centres but, by and large, women outlive and therefore outnumber men.

There are factors besides life expectancy hereabouts. For more than a hundred years, women and men of Highland Scots descent homesteaded, farmed and built businesses that made for a prosperous life in The Landing. Then, wars and the Great Depression decimated those farms and businesses as young men were killed or languished in veterans' institutions.

Men who remained struggled to make ends meet, working or drinking themselves to death. Their widows coped; sons moved away for work, and daughters sought careers in nursing, teaching and convents. One after another, the churches closed, then the school, as entire families migrated or died out.

With few young families calling The Landing home, the women of The Miller's Oven were keeping themselves busy and their village alive. They stuck together, supported each other and gave each other strength. In deference to the predominantly single or widowed elderly female staff, locals cheekily refer to the diner as "The Coven."

The restaurant occupies a 1950s wood-frame addition to a century-old former sawmill overlooking the once-thriving harbour that defined the village. But, like so many one-time anchors of rural economies, the aged timber buildings of the mill were no longer standing, except for one stone foundation wall that now forms the back of the diner's kitchen area. Opposite, drafty windows overlook the harbour and the abandoned ferry wharf.

That stone wall lends an air of authenticity to the enterprise, an air of permanence. Bolted to it, yellowed with dust and kitchen grease, is brandished a gigantic claymore, a double-edged sword favoured by Highland warriors in ages passed. More than a metre long, it hangs precariously over the butcher block counter that runs the length of that wall.

Here and there, cheap copies of paintings evoking chapters in Scottish history hang on the otherwise austere walls of the eating area. Random scenes of local industries, now defunct and invisible, punctuate the lesson.

Table six is situated between a faded copy of *Loch Aber No More* – a romanticized painting of Bonnie Prince Charlie's escape from Scotland after the Battle of Culloden in 1746 – and a ghostly photograph of mostly female workers outside the tannery that was once across the road.

Over my usual table are two portraits of women dressed in the Highland garb of tenacious femininity: one portrait is a fierce-looking woman brandishing a crossbow toward unseen assailants. "Black Agnes," says the caption, "That brawling boisterous Scottish wench (Sir Walter Scott)." The other is of the heroine Flora MacDonald who helped in the Bonnie Prince's escape.

There are more and similar images, large and small, throughout the room – mostly of women, mostly working, mostly vintage – and mostly underappreciated, as most patrons chose to sit by the windows for the view, despite the occasional draft.

∞∞

Under the watchful eyes of the women of the tannery, "his lordship" was reading the newspaper while waiting for his lunch. His wife, if that's who she was, sat quietly, hands almost imperceptibly worrying the white linen tablecloth that touched her lap.

"My mother called yesterday," I overheard her say quietly, "she wants us to come for a visit."

"Who?" asked the newspaper.

"Mother. She wants us to visit. Father is not well."

"He's old. What does she think you can do about it?" He emphasized 'you' rather pointedly.

"But he's not well, and my sister lives too far away to help."

"Not that she'd *be* much help."

The woman's demeanor put me in mind of the mouse I found live-trapped in the barn this morning – hunted, haunted, helpless – though I don't think the mouse's lower lip quivered in quite the same way.

"Not your fault, and not my problem." He lowered one corner of his newspaper so she would be sure to see him say, "you told her so, I presume."

"She doesn't understand." After a moment, she added, "I think he wants to see me before he dies."

"It's a little late for such pleasantries, don't you think?"

"It's not too late for forgiveness. He's dying."

"Your mother would say anything to get you to go over there – so she can say she told you so."

"It's not out of our way."

"I should have known better than to agree to come here for lunch. Fall colours indeed." He widened and flexed his arms to noisily return his newspaper to viewing distance. "You thought if we came this close, I'd give in. Well, I won't and you won't."

"I heard about this old place reopening and wanted to try it." Then, changing the subject, "they are old. They have no family or friends around here anymore. Everyone is gone from the glen. They're lonely and confused."

"They should have moved when they had the chance. Moved to town like everyone else, for Christ's sake. The smart ones, anyway. You were wrong about this place too."

Maggie delivered the Diet Pepsi and the water with a breezy, "I'll be right back with your lunches sweeties."

The woman smiled weakly in return. Her husband offered no acknowledgement.

Returning, Maggie placed the tuna sandwich in front of the man and the liver dinner in front of his wife with a smirk. "Here you go, dears."

As she turned away, he folded his newspaper roughly; a demeaning scowl registered the confusion. "'ere, you've got that wrong."

"Oh, that's right. Sorry hon." She exchanged the plates – in a rather exaggerated manner, I thought, and perhaps with a wry little smile.

"Are you sure you wouldn't like some dressing on your salad?" she asked.

"No," said his lordship in a manner which also said 'now go away.'

His lordship – as I now thought of him too – busied himself slashing and mashing his liver, onions, potatoes and peas to the consistency of pap. Whether the result of the effort or the earlier conversation, his chubby English cheeks and the tip of his puggish English nose were flushed cherry red.

Maggie came up brusquely, offering another Pepsi as she refilled the woman's water glass from a large plastic pitcher jingling with ice.

"No. Ice," he said disdainfully.

"It's alright," his wife reassured. "Thank you."

"Lovely afternoon," Maggie offered dutifully.

"God I hate these good-for-nothing little rubbish heaps," he said to the window after Maggie had moved to offer water to the next table. "The sooner they are all emptied out, the better. No roads to maintain, no pathetic appeals to preserve some forlorn, poverty-stricken way of life that isn't sustainable."

They lapsed into silence, except for his salivary smacking. She nibbled distractedly on her sandwich.

When it came time, Maggie tried to reoffer dessert. "How about that pie folks?"

She peered at the cooler across the room, going through an oral inventory with singsong familiarity:

Pecan, raisin
Coconut cream
Strawberry rhubarb
Apple with cream.
Mincemeat, cherry
Carrot cake too
Cheese plate, cheesecake
Fresh baked for you.

"Think about that, and I'll be right back."

"What part of 'no' does she not understand?" he asked rhetorically.

They were all looking now – the staff, that is. Prim grey heads nodded and wagged atop frilled aprons over tartan skirts and comfortable shoes at the far end of the service counter.

An annoyed look from table six interrupted their conflab, dispersing them to the four corners of the room. Once again they busied themselves with their customers or with some little detail in that way some waitresses have.

Maggie returned with two dessert plates. On one, a large piece of deep-dish mincemeat pie glistened invitingly; this she placed in front of him as though royalty. Whether it was the pie or the person getting the royal treatment, I couldn't say.

"On the 'ouse 'gov," she said in an exaggerated Cockney accent. "Last one in the fridge just lookin' for an 'owm, be it ever so 'umble. Wouldn't want it to go to wyste."

She placed a small plate with a single oatcake in front of the woman, refilled her tea, and with a quick flourish of her hand said, "local specialities, these." She turned on her heels and sped off.

Irrespective of his earlier refusals, the Englishman dove into the pie as though Maggie might change her mind and take it back.

"What?" Cheeks flushed from stuffing his face, he addressed his wife's look of surprise. "Can't let it go to waste." His wife didn't answer, just nibbled her oatcake and sipped her tea as though in contemplation.

When he finished, he wiped his mouth in an exaggerated fashion and pushed back his chair. "Going to the gents'," he told her hurriedly.

He quickly crossed the room toward the entrance in search of the toilets, only to find the gents' out of order.

"There's another in the basement," Maggie called across the room. "Mind the steps; we wouldn't want you to have a nasty fall!" Though the place was now less occupied, her co-workers seemed suddenly preoc-cupied.

Maggie crossed the room to table six to pick up the empty plates. "Would you like some more tea, dear? You look like you could use it."

"That would be nice. Thank you."

"You're not from around here," Maggie stated con-versationally when she returned with the tea. "I don't recall seeing you before."

"I am. Was. When I was younger. My parents live farther up the glen. I moved to the city when I got mar-ried."

"Who's your father?" Maggie asked in the time-honoured tradition.

"Chas Macdonald. Sometimes I wish I could be closer. He's not well. My father."

"Can't say I know them, but if they're from around here, they can't be all bad," Maggie laughed. "You picked the right time of year for a visit, it's beautiful here in the fall. How come you don't visit more often?"

"My husband doesn't get along with them," then she whispered quickly, "they never liked him."

"No kidding!" Maggie said without thinking, then quickly added, "well now, dearie, you never know what the future holds, do ye? Maybe you'll be happy to come back to stay someday."

It came time for me to leave – I had recently sworn off desserts – and I called to Maggie for my bill, paid her and left the diner before his lordship had returned to his seat.

∞∞

Billowing white cumulous clouds in the blue October sky set off the brilliant yellow, orange and red autumn leaves that punctuated passing glimpses of Loch Bras d'Or as I made my way toward Marble Mountain and beyond.

I couldn't help thinking about the cloud that seemed to hang over the unhappy strangers. Funny how some people stick in your mind and your craw; his lordship was certainly one of those. "That poor woman – stuck with that A-hole," I thought out loud. Funny what some people put up with."

Maybe I was just put off by his lordship's pompous English accent. Local resentment toward the English runs rather deeper than is reasonable around here. Maybe her father was one of those old-time Scots who never got over losing their livelihoods to English land-owners. Geez, that was more than 200 years and five generations ago!

It was none of my business, but – friggin' bully. Lulled to other matters by the scenery and the deplorable road conditions, my mind wandered, and they were forgotten.

∞∞

A few weeks later, Maggie greeted me as I entered the diner, signalling me to take my usual table by the window. She followed, waving a fresh pot of coffee.

"The new girl will be over to take your order in a few minutes hon." She nodded over her shoulder to the serving area. "Moved back home a couple of weeks ago. Mary Margaret. She's a Macdonald, from back the glen."

fin

MAC TALLA / THE ECHO

"**M**oney doesn't grow on trees, you know!"

Egads, I sound like my father. I've channelled him before, telling our children that 'no,' we were not going to spend precious money on the latest devices by which they can further ignore us. Egads, I said "egads!"

We try not to use outdated recriminations on our grandchildren – despite the fact that their next-generation digital distractions are now beyond our comprehension. Kids have lots of time for watching TikTok videos or for fleeting gossip on Snapchat, but no time to sit with their elders, even at mealtime. These days, time might be an even more precious resource than money – something I only recently started to pay attention to – giving meaning to another of my father's overused parentisms: "time is money."

References to the importance of time to children are many: time out; time's up; waste of time; time waits for no one; the time has come; time to reap and time to sow; bedtime; overtime. It would not be a stretch in our current state of affairs to mash up those two overused sayings to say: "Time doesn't grow on trees, you know."

Except when it does.

∞∞

Just such a conflict struck close to home a few years ago when my dad died unexpectedly. Well, it wasn't so much unexpected as we were unprepared. Old people die. He was old. What was unexpected, however, was the heart attack – not his, mine.

It would be a stretch to say that it – the heart at-tack – was the best thing that ever happened to me, but it *was* a wake-up call, one that I needed, and one that I heeded.

My father grew up here in The Landing. Like doz-ens of places in Cape Breton, The Landing got smaller and smaller during the last century, though unlike places that have all but disappeared, The Landing is still here and still home to descendants of the early settlers, the Highland Gaels – though we are fewer and older. The village shrank until it no longer suited my dad's generation, and most moved away.

In one of those coincidences that Maritimers love to recount, my parents met at a dance in Toronto, which is where my mother grew up. Her parents, my Toronto grandparents, were actually from The Landing too but had left the area in disgrace – some sort of falling out over religion, or politics, or property inheritance or something. If the subject ever came up among the elders, the conversation would switch to Gaelic, their mother tongue, and the younger generations would be left out.

Neither my mother nor her parents ever visited The Landing. The only tangible connection my mother had with her family was a faded tin-type photo of her grandparents – my great grandparents. In that picture, the dour pair were posing near the doorway of a smallish shingled frame house – she seated at a rickety-looking spinning wheel, he seated next to her, holding an ancient set of Highland bagpipes.

In retirement, my parents moved to The Landing to live in my father's father's house. Mom died some years later, leaving Dad to keep the homefires burning. My Toronto-born wife and two kids and I made the long drive from Toronto to spend vacation time in the summers. When my dad died, and I was advised to retire, the empty house in a rural setting seemed just what the doctor ordered, so we took it over.

The old place wasn't much to look at, but it has good bones and a good heart. Once we got rid of some of the worn-out furniture and cranberry-glass goblets my grandmother had collected, and after refurbishing and refurnishing, my wife and I settled into a comfortable existence.

I'm a romantic at heart. Out here in The Landing, the history envelopes you. The ghosts speak to you. The area was once populated almost exclusively by Gaels. For more than a hundred years – almost two hundred now – small farms and orchards lined the spaces between the mountains behind us and the loch in front. For more than a hundred years, Gaelic and Mi'kmaw were spoken in these parts. But in the hundred years since – neither. Once a bustling, industrious lochside town, there are now more overgrown stone foundations and fallen fences than there are occupied homes. Only ghosts tend the now-feral orchards.

My father never learned it, the Gaelic, nor did my mother; I didn't have any interest beyond the few pat phrases spoken in front of tourists and at funerals. None of my friends spoke it, even if their parents or grandparents did. To my discredit, I was proud of my Highland roots but, like countless of my generation, not proud enough to do anything in earnest about it beyond those phrases and beyond singing along with Irish drinking songs thinking they sounded about right.

As a youngster I did learn to play the bagpipes, after a fashion – which is to say 'not very well.' I even played in a marching pipe band for awhile. The band helped to obscure my lack of talent, but it made my mother proud to see me all kilted out and marching smartly in formation in the cold rain of Remembrance Day parades.

There is a fair amount of interest in Celtic cultures in urban areas – Highland dancing and marching pipe bands – though purists call it tokenism. People fetishize bagpipes, kilts and their imitation sealskin sporrans, and they cheer on "Address to a Haggis" at Robbie Burns suppers. But they don't go much beyond that or beyond displaying their well-worn copies of *A Forest for Calum* and *No Great Mischief* under family pictures on an end table in the parlour.

To my regret in maturity, my adolescent years in the city traded marching in skirts for chasing skirts, and the pipes were abandoned. Then came kids and dogs and – you get the idea.

My parents, bless them, had kept my abandoned bagpipes. When we took over the house we found them, still in their case among a jumble of old suitcases, trunks and cartons in the attic.

You can see where this is going: old history, old house, old heart, old pipes.... One slight problem. As an adult I couldn't carry a tune in a bag, let alone coax a tune out of one again. But I had as a kid so, looking for some sort of cultural hobby, I decided to try.

I bought instruction videos, watched endless YouTube concerts and amateur instruction clips, and listened in rapture to massed pipes CDs in preparation. Alone in the shed I practised, like the videos said, on a practice chanter. It was like learning a new language. And, like learning a new language, I was a long time working up the courage to try chanter and bag, then to try it out on anyone.

It turned out that I wasn't quite ready to give a house concert, for the first was also the last. There is a little-known codicil to the marriage vows, a footnote to "in sickness and in health, 'til death do us part": that codicil reads, "no allowances made for bagpipe-playing in the matrimonial home." There's an old joke that 'a gentleman knows how to play the bagpipes, and doesn't.' My wife suggested that if I wanted to commune with my ancestors, I take up genealogy or get a Ouija board.

∞∞

The dog returned after a couple of days alright, but I'm still not allowed to play in the house. I did manage to claim a corner of the shed as my own and kept up the learning and playing. I took lessons from old Wally Ellison over in West Bay Road. He was much more patient than my wife and her dog. Wally even got me trying to learn some Gaelic. He said knowing some would help me 'get' the music better, referring several times to playing in the old style – though I never learned for certain what he meant by that.

I also started playing while walking, thinking it might reconnect me with my pipe band days. Sometimes I paced and played on the deer trails behind the house, sometimes along the shoreline around the cove once I thought I was a little better.

I've not seen or heard it expressed, but the pipes have the curious effect of both *evoking* and *assuaging* isolation. Does that make sense? Whether it's completely natural or complete nonsense, I couldn't say, but my romantic self – the inner Gael, maybe – came to see my solitary parades as time in the bank of life, and I don't care who knows it.

I found it odd that no one else in the village commented on my solo concerts. I didn't think they were that bad. But as far as I could tell, I was playing only to the geese and gulls that call The Landing home. I'm not *really* saying that the birds could relate to me or my music, but I took comfort in the fact that they didn't fly away.

Wally once told me that the Gaelic was more nature-oriented than the English. He said that the beauty of the Gaelic is that it's infused with the landscape. I guess that's why the early Gaelic-speaking immigrants got along so well with the Mi'kmaq, they shared respect for the land on which they were dependent, and it comes out in their languages. I'll always remember a saying he quoted: 'The earth has music for those who listen.' He didn't know who said it first, Shakespeare maybe, though I later learned that it wasn't.

Quite often, depending on the weather, when I paused between tunes, the final refrain would echo from the hills across the loch. It was like a faraway piper, a faerie piper, was playing along – or perhaps mocking me, depending on my mood or level of self-confidence in the moment. My reading of piping lore often recounted stories of pipers 'receiving' tunes in dreams or from faeries. In my imagination, it was the trees and the distant corrie that influenced the natural flourishes I was incorporating.

I took my time, and I listened, revelling in nature's revisions, respecting them, practising them, growing my feel for the tunes, perfecting my piping vocabulary by letting nature into my technique. I was chuffed by the realization that I was incrementally adding 'dirt' to my playing. 'Dirt' is an expression used by fiddlers and pipers alike for the flutters and flourishes added spontaneously to a tune – extra notes and half-notes that showcase a player's mastery. Nature's echo helped me find my dirt. Wally said I was slowly getting the old style.

∞∞

But the echo stopped, which I found peculiar. Whenever the wind was from the north the pipes hadn't answered, of course, but this was different. Something in the landscape had changed; there was no answering refrain, not even on a calm, crisp evening.

That silence may have contributed to my decision to try to form an interest group, a sort of piping circle. Maybe it was a vain desire to hear myself echoed again. I don't know. I wasn't so cocky as to think I would teach something I had only recently learned, but I was so high on what I had accomplished through the application of time and patience that I wanted to share it with others. It would be more of a social thing.

More important, I wanted to be part of a revival. There seems less interest in the old ways and music in these parts in these days, which is paradoxical. In town, there was plenty of interest. Here in the heart of the once-vibrant language and custom that I was rediscovering and honouring, almost nothing. The old-timers are gone, the language all but forgotten; only the music remains, and, sadly, that too could fade if no one makes time for it.

So, I made up an announcement and took it to the post office.

∞∞

I don't know how we manage to still have a real post office in The Landing. There seems hardly enough people to support it, though the numbers of seasonal residents are increasing. The post office is a throwback to past times but vital to preserving life in the area. It's a social hitching post where people take a little time, catch up

on local news, meet long-unseen neighbours, and seek
or offer help in exchange.

The Landing's post office has an overflowing bul-
letin board, of course. Faded pieces of paper advertise
lawn mowing and snow removal, firewood, fresh honey
or tailoring, lemonade stands and meals-on-wheels
alongside benefits, bingo and bake sales. I surveyed
the notices to find something out of date that I could
remove or cover over and was surprised to find a small,
soiled card that I had not noticed before. In an elderly
hand it read:

piper wanted

for memorial

should have the old style

saturday morning

the tanneries

An audition? How many pipers did they think were
around here? Memorial for whom? Remembrance Day
was still months away.

I tacked up my own poster and chatted with the
postmaster, Joanie, until the next person came in for
their mail. Making my excuses when others arrived, I
left without remembering to ask who had posted about
the audition.

Days later, during my next visit to the post office, I
was reminded of the call for a piper. The audition was
the next day, just up the road at the Tanneries Tavern, a
snug, if dingy, pub from another time overlooking the
cove that defined the village.

∞∞

In a darkened corner of the room, the now-uncommon
smell of stale tobacco located the only other living
occupants. A slight, elderly man in a yellowed tweed

jacket sat next to the tavern's smouldering fireplace. In front of him, a small table sported a glass of golden liquid – whisky, no doubt. On the chair beside him was a dusty set of ancient-looking pipes. At his feet, a grey-whiskered collie dog looked up at my approach, cocking its head quizzically.

The linguistic limit of all but a few people, a greeting in Gaelic is almost mandatory around here. "*Ciamar a tha thu?*" I asked. How are you?

"*Tha mi gu math, tapadh leat. Ciamar a tha thu-fhein?*" the old fellow replied in kind. Then in English, "Well enough, thank you. How are you yourself? You have the Gaelic?" he asked, though he undoubtedly knew the answer.

"To my shame," I replied. "Just a few phrases." .

"Pity. Did you come to play?"

His tired eyes assessed my every move as I unpacked my case and began to assemble my pipes – which I did slowly and deliberately, assuming that we'd soon be joined by others, maybe a committee. The collie raised itself with its forelegs, eyes bright in recognition. Ears cocked, it looked from me to its master and back in anticipation.

"What's your name, uncle?" I asked respectfully.

"Mac an tòisich. McIntosh."

"Like the mountain?" I asked, nodding toward the rear of the pub.

"Aye."

A man of few words.

"My mother's people were McIntosh," I said. The old boy shifted a bit in his seat but didn't engage me on the point.

To put us both at ease – especially me, for it felt a bit like I was applying for a job smuggling drugs or something – I pulled a rickety wooden chair closer to attempt more small talk and to await the call to play. My eyes followed his look to the scene beyond the pub windows – to the sandy point that sheltered the cove from the greater waters of the loch.

"Lived here a long time?" I prodded.

"Not long enough." His eyes twinkled at his little joke, then repeated, more seriously, "not long enough."

Even from that brief exchange, I could detect the lilting accent so prevalent here in Inverness County. The dialect is carried over from the days when the Gaelic dominated. If not the vocabulary, the manner of speaking runs deep.

Seated nearer, I could study him better in the dim light. He appeared small and vulnerable beneath his ill-fitting tweed. Old people shrink in time. He hadn't shaved in a few days – not uncommon among elderly men without women to press them to get cleaned up once in awhile. Wisps of white hair on the nape of his neck were in need of a trim. Maybe this memorial thing was for his late wife?

Tapping a silent tune on the table next to the whisky, if that's what it was, his dirty fingernails capped knotty nicotine-stained fingers. An unlit cigarette lay beside a wrinkled pack on the table. Ashes dusted his jacket and his lap.

"Do you play?" I asked, patting the jumble of pipe pieces in my lap.

"Yes. No. Not anymore. No wind for it. Couldn't blow to save my life." He absentmindedly reached down to scratch between the dog's ears. Its tail twitched briefly in appreciation of the attention. The dog's claws were long and soiled like the old man's.

"Time for someone else to play," he said.

"I played as a boy but only recently started taking it seriously." Then, trying to be deferential, I added, "still trying to get it right."

"You play well enough for a beginner," he said. In response to my quizzical look, he nodded toward the windows and added, "heard you in the cove."

"I play whenever I have time to spare."

"Time is hard to come by."

"We hope living here will make a difference."

"Don't waste it, your time." His long, dirty nails rasped through his whiskers pensively. I hoped "waste" wasn't referring to my musical efforts.

Taught not to stare, and worried what my gaze might reveal, I stood up, arranged the pipes on my shoulder and massaged the bag purposefully.

"Mind if I practice a bit?" I asked. "Do you have a favourite?"

"'Cha Till MacCriumein,' 'MacCrimmon Will Never Return'."

"No kidding! That's an old one. I've tried it a few times myself. Difficult fingering."

He looked me over, eyes twinkling from beneath the dullness of age. "Think you got it right?"

"Only you and I will know," I chuckled, "and maybe the collie there. They need someone to play for a service?"

"If you get it right."

"You won't join me?"

"I canna' play no more. My time is up."

His melancholia gave sudden clarity. "You're it? No one else is coming? I'm it?"

"We'll see."

∞∞

I played "Lochaber No More," a lament.

Man, how I played! But he hardly budged. Didn't even crack a smile or tap a foot the whole time – which is unusual; people around here tap their feet in time with church music. He just sat there glassy-eyed, staring out the windows.

Just before the last breath left the drones, he leaned forward a little, so I picked up the pace, and lit up "Tulloch Gorm," a Strathspey, followed by "Muileann Dubh" to make it a set.

Time spent practising, listening and growing with the music was paying off. There was no echo in here, but I could feel the music come back at me and through me from every corner. The many-paned windows fairly rattled; the room surely expanded and contracted with each breath as though the roof might blow. *Suas è*, they say around here – drivin'er – if I do say so myself.

I wanted to please that crusty old fellow like it was Judgement Day. Mine or his, I couldn't say. I wanted him to feel the music that he no longer made for himself. But there was no emotion on his part. Not much anyway. When it was over, the collie exhaled loudly before tiredly settling its snout back on the hardwood.

"You can play." McIntosh nodded at the glass of whisky deliberately, somewhat formally. "Pay for the Piper," he said.

Ceremoniously, pipes cradled in my elbow, I took the dram and downed half of it before indicating that he should finish it, as was the custom.

McIntosh hitched himself to one side of his chair as if to reach for his purse.

"Paid," I said, waving off his gesture. "Piper's paid."

Nodding appreciation and respect, he resumed his seated position but did not touch the glass.

"One piper for another," I said in mock salute. Then I took the glass and emptied it for him.

"Saturday," he said. As he did, he nodded to bring my attention to a yellowed piece of paper I'd not noticed behind the glass.

∞∞

Saturday, as requested, I hauled my old pipes and my old arse up the old mountain road to the coordinates written on the paper. Not an address per se, I found myself on the edge of a nearly overgrown cemetery plot overlooking a likewise overgrown homestead. Lilac bushes marked where succeeding generations of outdoor privies once stood.

There was no one else around. I checked my watch to see if I was maybe early or, god forbid, late. To my credit, I was early, and to bide my time, I strolled about the weedy plots. Most headstones, ancient alongside old, were worn on their way to oblivion like their charges laid beneath – MacKay, Ross, MacDonald, McIntosh – family names of early settlers from Scotland whose time had run out here at The Landing.

The headstones, each alone in their togetherness, bore witness to the passage of generations, standing for those who no longer stood. In that moment, I was the only breathing witness. I paused by a weedy depression in front of a newish granite marker obviously laid in more recent times.

IN MEMORY OF OUR ANCESTOR
RUADH MCINTOSH
THE FAERIE PIPER

Laser-etched in the polished stone were two oval portraits: a set of Highland bagpipes and a handsome collie dog.

I played my best that day, and I didn't let up after just one set either. I played as though my life depended on it – as though time stood still.

fin

POOR WOOLLY AND THE BEAR

Meet Poor Woolly

Born William MacAulay, the name Willie suited him better as a lad, which people around here pronounce more like Wullie. That morphed to Woolly at a young age, a reference to his head of wiry black hair. Woolly is not too swift, some say; lacking wit, some say. Woolly headed, they say. His conversational style is off-putting to those who make too much of talking and not enough of listening.

Most regard him as a bit addled, if not downright slow, and he's treated as such by most in that demeaning way that some people have. That little shake of the head and double-click of the tongue – 'tsk, tsk, poor Woolly.' Everyone in The Landing has referred to him as Poor Woolly for so long he answers to it.

"What a day!" The sun was just beginning to show itself to the north mountain in a sky as blue as Poor Woolly had seen it in ages. "On a day like this...." He paused, then decided to leave the thought open to see what the day would bring. There was energy in the air, but that did not quicken his deliberate pace. He didn't wish to arrive in The Landing before the sunlight warmed it.

It was Tuesday. On Tuesday, Poor Woolly goes into the village to get his mail and supplies.

Poor Woolly hitched his worn leather satchel more securely on his shoulder. Comforted by the weight of its contents safely intact, he rounded the turn by the village green. There, at regular intervals, are held picnics, gospel meetings, the county fair, sports and homecomings – events that change the character of the whole village, if only for a few hours.

This week, it would be the circus. Poor Woolly preferred to visit in the morning, when circus folks were not in such a hurry, when he could meet them and talk with them, and they with him. He'd not actually been to the circus in the evening when things were in high gear. He imagined it would be like the county fair – too busy, too noisy, too dazzling. Too confusing. The blinking lights, the blaring music and the shouting were just too much for him. In the daytime, he could enjoy the characters and the animals without worrying for his safety. He could just imagine the rest.

He had almost been to a city circus once. In the city where his sister lives. He didn't like it much, the city, that is.

One day when they were in her car and stuck in traffic, she smacked the wheel in frustration and yelled "what a G-D circus!" But on account of the traffic, they never actually got to one. He never got to see the rat race either. That whole visit was traumatic, and he never went back, though she invited him. She never visited him in The Landing anymore either, now that their parents were gone, but he understood. She was probably stuck in traffic.

"Good morning Woolly." Skeleton Lady nodded to him and smiled as he turned the corner by her trailer. He blushed. Poor Woolly thought she was very attractive, and he always blushed when they crossed paths. She was standing outside, talking and laughing with Fat Man.

Fat Man made Poor Woolly blush too, but more because he was embarrassed for him. His clothes didn't fit, and his large hairy belly hung so far below his shirt you could only see his legs below the knees. Still, he was friendly, jolly even, and always had a nod and a smile for everyone – though Poor Woolly quickly looked away. As long as he was healthy and happy, his size didn't really matter. When Fat Man laughed, his belly jiggled in all directions, like the fat white pine tree outside the post office. The tree branches undulate madly in all directions when it was windy.

It was a very inviting day. Almost everyone on the north side of the lane had their place wide open already. Stopping in front of the doorway of Tattoo Man, Poor Woolly could see him engaged in lively conversation with Countess, one of the lady clowns.

"Goot morgan Voolly," she smiled and waved. At least, she probably smiled. He couldn't really tell on account of her makeup. Her garish face paint made for an exaggerated smile, and Poor Woolly couldn't really tell what she was thinking. Her strange accent made her rather exotic. She didn't sound like most people around here, whose Gaelic-speaking ancestors had left traces of their infectious sing-song dialect in local expression.

Though Tattoo Man had eyes on the back of his head, it was Countess's greeting that made him turn and greet Poor Woolly with a broad smile and a wave of his colourful hand. He had no hair, none on his head, his face, his arms, or his leg – he only had one leg, and he always wore short trousers so you could see that. Poor Woolly figured that because Tattoo Man hadn't any hair, he covered himself with ink instead.

Poor Woolly's late uncle had tattoos – the Virgin Mary on his left forearm and a barenaked lady on his right. He'd only been to church three times in his life, but he was in the navy for years. When anyone asked him about the Virgin Mary, he would give a saucy wink and a nod, first to his left, then his right, saying, "she changed her name after she met me."

"Good morning Woolly!" Across the lane, Strong Man was walking World's Ugliest Dog. Poor Woolly thought World's Ugliest Dog looked a lot like a pig, but he never questioned the Strong Man on that for obvious reasons. Strong Man was the opposite of Fat Man, though like Tattoo Man, he was hairless. He had a square jaw and the broadest smile of the whitest most perfect teeth of anyone Poor Woolly had ever seen.

To accommodate all those perfect teeth in that too-perfect smile, his upper lip formed a kind of snarl. The contrast was confusing – like a barking dog wagging its tail. Perhaps Strong Man and his ugly dog spent so much time together that they were starting to look alike, a mental picture that made Poor Woolly smile inside.

"H'lo pooch," he said, though he knew the dog had a name. People sometimes give animals names, but he found that rather silly. Imagine if he'd given people-names to the forest animals around his cabin – the thought made him shake his head.

World's Ugliest Dog let out a short "woof," turning half around to look through the dusty gap between Tattoo Man's stand and that of Ballerina. It sounded like there was a pack of dogs just out of sight, maybe chasing something, maybe a bunny.

The circus had quite a few dogs of various sizes and breeds – all of which were exceptionally smart, in Poor Woolly's estimation. They could perform all manner of tricks when he let them think he had treats in his pockets. He hoped nothing happened to the bunny, if that's what they were chasing.

He had a soft spot for bunnies. He used to call them rabbits, but Human Encyclopedia once informed him there were no rabbits in Cape Breton, only hares. Hares doesn't exactly roll off the tongue – you wouldn't say you had hare stew for supper – so Poor Woolly started saying bunnies, like he was still a child. Secretly, he knew for a fact that there were rabbits in Cape Breton because he had seen them in cages at the county fair. Human Encyclopedia said those didn't count.

Poor Woolly always looked the other way when he passed Ballerina. He was embarrassed by the flimsy costumes she wore, even when she wasn't dancing or swinging from her platform. Human Encyclopedia called her skirt a tutu, and Poor Woolly understood. It was too short, too thin, too pink. Other men didn't seem to mind. Tattoo Man often stood with his crutches outside her door from where he could chat with her while keeping an eye on his own place. Poor Woolly was sure that Tattoo Man spoke differently with Ballerina than with anyone else, including Countess. He wasn't sure he could explain the difference – it was just a feeling he had.

Poor Woolly looked at his watch, though he was pretty sure it was 9 o'clock because, just then, Ringmaster made an appearance like always – right on time. He came down the three steps of his trailer to the dusty lane, stopped, and took out his golden watch on its golden chain attached to his vest pocket.

Ringmaster always wore a three-piece suit, even in the daytime. It was soiled and shiny in places, the shoulders dusted by white flecks and fallen hairs. His ponderous belly stretched the vest to its limit, but he looked grand.

He stared at his watch for what seemed to Poor Woolly to be an unnecessarily long time. Poor Woolly had once heard Bossy Clown make a joke about the watch while having tea with a group of the other lady clowns. It must have been a joke because they all laughed – he didn't actually get it, something about the way Ringmaster fondled his watch.

The moment Ringmaster snapped his watch closed, Bossy Clown and her friend Big Balloons appeared around the corner. Bossy always moved like she had to be somewhere important, and Big Balloons always looked uncomfortable – kind of bent forward at the waist as if a little off balance. She always walked as though trying to keep up with herself, and today she kept going straight when Bossy turned sharply to go around Ringmaster.

Poor Woolly noticed that something was amiss with Bossy's makeup today. She seemed unfinished. Ringmaster must have noticed too, for his eyes followed her particularly closely, with the same moon-eyed look on his face that Tattoo Man had for Ballerina.

Usually, Ringmaster and Bossy exchanged a few words, but she was very animated today. Mumbling something about Skeleton Lady, she brushed right by Poor Woolly without a word. Ringmaster shrugged and went back up the steps, inside and out of sight.

On days like this, Poor Woolly liked to sit on a bench across from the cove. And because it was such a lovely morning, many animals were about with their humans, perhaps while their cages were being cleaned. He watched them as they stretched their legs under the watchful eyes of circus folk.

Poor Woolly could tell that the animals didn't really like each other by the way they sniffed in curiosity and suspicion, but surely they were used to each other by now. Surely there was no risk of a fight – a few snorts and growls, maybe, but not a fight – at least, he hoped not.

Tony, the tiger, paced in deliberate strides back and forth along the edge of the water studying his reflection. So long confined, Poor Woolly thought, Tony was starved for company.

At the other end of the grassy area bordering the cove, the baby elephant, Edward, walked in an ever-widening spiral until his human called on him to return. Deeply distracted, Edward walked back to a middle point that only he could see and started the spiral again. Even as he walked his body swayed compulsively back and forth, back and forth, as if to some silent symphony. Poor Woolly felt a special connection with Edward.

More of the circus was coming alive; more characters were stepping out into the warmth now that the sun was fully in the sky. They were always kind to him, the circus folk. Ringmaster once told him that everyone felt a special connection with him and other people like him – whatever that meant.

Only once had he been treated badly, which was just a misunderstanding. He used to spend quite a bit of time with Ice Cream Man, who had his stand open all the time, not just at night. Poor Woolly got to know quite a bit about ice cream by watching him serve customers. One busy day Ice Cream Man asked Poor Woolly to watch the stand for a few minutes. A man and his two children wanted ice creams, and since Poor Woolly thought he knew how to do it and how much to charge and how to make change, he served them.

Well! Ice Cream Man was so upset! He said all manner of mean things and accused Poor Woolly of stealing, and he put the run on him. It was embarrassing. And confusing. Poor Woolly was just trying to help. In fact, he was sure Ice Cream Man had asked him to help.

Ringmaster heard that racket and came to Poor Woolly's aid, calming him. Much later, Ice Cream Man apologized, but it was never the same between them; he still avoided the Keystone Cop clowns out of fear that Ice Cream Man might have complained.

A shrill warning buzzer sounded behind him, and Poor Woolly quickly turned to look up the street. It was 10 o'clock. After only a moment, a door burst open releasing a clamour of monkeys so filled with pent-up energy they almost flew to the perimeter of the cage that prevented them from pouring onto the road.

One or two of the little monkeys attempted to climb the fence, while others variously chased each other in circles or chased a soccer ball. The running and the jumping and the high-pitched chatter were great fun to watch; Poor Woolly almost wished he could join in. He couldn't, of course. He'd been warned to keep his distance. Bossy Clown had once said it would be inappropriate.

Exercise period didn't last long – fifteen minutes, maybe. The buzzer sounded again, and the monkeys abruptly stopped what they were doing, lined up at the door and waited to be led back inside. Playtime was over. It was feeding time. 'They are so well trained!' Poor Woolly shook his head in amusement and turned once again to face the sun and the water.

"Mornin' Woolly," called a rough but cheery voice close behind him.

"Yes—" Poor Woolly's greeting caught in his throat as he turned and came face-to-face with ... Bear! The Bear!

Poor Woolly's eyes went so wide his heart might have jumped right out had it not been lodged throbbing in his throat. He hated being this close to Bear. And he had never heard Bear speak before. Its slimy nostrils twitched as it studied Poor Woolly, who worried he had stopped breathing altogether.

"She won't hurt you, Woolly. You know that." Bear's lips weren't moving, but her nostrils twitched, now oozing snot. Little puffs of its breath tickled Poor Woolly's eyelashes. Deep brown eyes stared out at him from under brows raised in expectation. The chain around Bear's neck – disconcertingly slack, in Poor Woolly's opinion – sparkled as the links rattled in the sunlight.

Mr. Trainer, who was Bear's constant companion, was standing close beside her. He smiled with familiarity and made an extra reassuring loop of the chain around his wrist.

"Sorry, Woolly. We saw you here, and she wanted to say hello."

Mr. Trainer smiled apologetically as Bear fussed and snorted for Poor Woolly's attention. He was more nervous around Bear than any of the other animals, despite Mr. Trainer's assurances. Poor Woolly's father had always emphasized that an animal is an animal, no matter how well trained, no matter how well behaved and friendly, no matter how well-meaning its human.

"H-hello Bear," Poor Woolly said, trying to use the critter-friendly voice he used when speaking to most of the animals in his forest. Not the bears, though. He had a deep-seated fear of bears.

Bear sniffed aggressively around Poor Woolly's satchel and his jacket and his trousers pockets, leaving a slimy trail as she did. Poor Woolly often had treats and was generally good to share.

"What's new in your world, Woolly?" asked Mr. Trainer as if there was nothing to worry about. "What are you reading these days?"

Poor Woolly spent a lot of time reading. He didn't have a lot of books, but he read a lot – rereading his favourites often and enjoying them anew. He took the same books in turn from the post office library time and time again. He had for years. It was a source of teasing by some in The Landing, but Mr. Trainer was different. He knew Poor Woolly could and did read a lot – just not a lot of variety.

"Don't let those folks bother you," Mr. Trainer once reassured him. "None of them read more than obituaries and gossip columns."

Poor Woolly took a book from his leather satchel and held it out. *The Greatest Shows on Earth.*

"Ah. The circus, is it?" Poor Woolly didn't need to answer because it was obvious. Neither said more.

Breaking the silence after a moment, Mr. Trainer jingled Bear's chain. "We're off, then." He tugged at Bear's lead who gave Poor Woolly one last great snort, turned, and pulled Mr. Trainer away up the lane.

Poor Woolly stretched in relief, looking up and down the lane as he did. He could walk forever, but sitting made him stiff.

"*Maduinn mhath*, Woolly." Joanie, the postmaster, called to him as she crossed the lane toward the little green house that served as The Landing's post office. Poor Woolly picked up his satchel from the bench and followed.

While Joanie put down the coffee she carried on the counter, Poor Woolly went to the bookcase under the stairs where he slid *The Greatest Shows on Earth* into a slack place in the top row. Then, moving his fingertips delicately along the spines of the other books as though he could read the contents through the bindings, he made his choice and turned back to the counter where Joanie was double-checking his mail. Flyers and a card from their MP.

"What will you read this week, Woolly?" Joanie asked, acknowledging the book he was putting in his satchel. Withdrawing it again, he showed her.

"*Gulliver's Travels*," she read aloud. "Jonathan Swift. One of my favourites."

"One of my favourites," Poor Woolly agreed.

∞∞

A few hours later, after tea with his friend Kenzie, Poor Woolly began to make his way back up the hill from the village. The afternoon sun was starting to lengthen his shadow. Stopping for a moment outside the church to adjust the bag of groceries Kenzie had brought from town, Poor Woolly reflected on his day so far.

Despite the encounter with Bear, he'd found his favourite people and animals entertaining. With a gentle squeeze of his elbow on the satchel to be sure that *Gulliver's Travels* was safely inside, he resumed his pace, thinking ahead to the characters he would meet next week. Next Tuesday.

fin

DICK AND JANE (AND BARBIE)

This is the story of the Christmas to end all Christmases, at least for Dick and Jane.

"I never had a Barbie," Jane said without turning toward Dick from her wing-back chair. The television was extolling the virtues of the latest iconic girl-toy, Scandinavian Safari Barbie. Or maybe it was Sorority Barbie or something like that. Dick wasn't too clear on the finer points of this particular new doll.

Most of the time, TV ads are just a distraction, a nuisance of noise and pictures. It's true that they can spark discussion, sometimes an argument. But sometimes, they border on epiphanies. That was the case for our hero, Dick. That's because, in keeping with the TV's not-so-subtle reminders, Christmas was approaching.

Dick was paying a little more attention to the many possibilities among the adult-oriented ads for something Jane might appreciate. It was their twentieth Christmas together and her fiftieth year, so gift-giving seemed particularly important this year. Dick was definitely paying attention.

It was still a couple of months before Christmas, and the idiot box (the television, that is) was alive with advertisements steering consumers this way and that toward making their gift-buying decisions. From Lego to Lite-Brite, from Mechano sets to Monopoly games, and Pick-up Sticks to Karaoke machines, the Christmas gift choices were seemingly endless.

For the third time that evening – among reruns of *Murder She Wrote* and *Third Rock from the Sun* – Barbie was being flogged. Not flogged in the Biblical sense, of course, but in the manner of repetitive retail reinforcement.

Dick knew that Jane's family was cash-poor when she and her siblings were children on the farm, but he hadn't realized that she had been deprived. He saw Jane in an entirely new light and locked onto the revelation.

He should have known, of course. She was smart, strong, independent – tough, even. No nonsense. No conforming to gendered stereotypes, she was a good lover and a good mother. And very real. Decidedly non-Barbie. Not that playing with dolls absolutely reinforces gender expectations. That's an oversimplification.

But Dick and Jane's relationship had seen better days. Things were strained – not that they'd discussed it, of course – and something in him seized upon her Barbie-less childhood. It was something he could fix.

Because Dick's man-brain could only hold open one door at a time, accessing the perfect Barbie became his fixation. It would be the perfect gift to show Jane that he'd heard her. The perfect gift to show her his romantic side, his thoughtful side, his spousal sensitivity. This year, this Christmas, Jane would get her long overdue Barbie doll.

∞∞

Feminism warned us about gendered toys like Barbie and of Mattel's unrealistic vision of the ideal North American female form. Of course, we can't intelligently attribute femininity to playing with dolls any more than playing with action figures (dolls for boys) and toy guns causes people to pursue paramilitary careers – or become mass murderers.

He recognized the hypocrisy, but couldn't do otherwise. He had to buy Jane her first Barbie, and he could justify it by reminding himself that you can't blame Barbie for society's views of femininity and the objectification of women. Just as you can't blame toy guns for all gun violence.

Dick actually considered himself a feminist – he often said so. He also acted it in the things he thought, said and did. For Dick, gender equality remained an important goal for society. We've come a long way, he'd often say to the guys at the tavern, but not far enough.

Playing with dolls does not a doll make. Dick understood that. He really did. If he didn't then, he does now. He knew the difference. Hurrah for pink Lego and lavender tool belts!

Yet, he had to seek out and acquire a Barbie for Jane for Christmas – her first Barbie. Finding the right Barbie became Dick's mission for the year. That mission: to satisfy her childhood unfulfilled; to show that he did listen sometimes; to show his romantic side, his insight, his thoughtfulness, his male sensitivities. Such a gift would make it clear. He'd fill that gap in her childhood.

∞∞

Not just any Barbie would do. It had to be a special-occasion Barbie. Unique, elegant, independent. Maybe a limited-edition Barbie. Not ironing-board Barbie, but executive Barbie. Not swimsuit Barbie like his sister's, that he so admired as a boy. Not back seat Barbie, but driver's seat Barbie. How about crane operator Barbie?

I don't know how many men have shopped for that one special Barbie in recent years. The toy departments have lots of pink Lego and Lavender tool belts, but feminine-idol dolls, like Barbie, are getting harder and harder to find. It's as though some great shame of association has descended upon the toy nation. Barbie, it seems, has been culled by retail self-monitoring and moralizing.

Shop after shop, clerk after clerk, a trail of lesser-than dolls in his wake, Dick found that shopping for a Barbie doll was a double-edged sword. The sword of dignity, which he had hoped to brandish as he came to the rescue of their relationship, became a problem.

He cut himself a little on that sword. The closer it got to Christmas, dignity shifted closer to indignity. His prolonged presence in the little girls' toy section sometimes elicited more than a few glances of concern.

Shop after shop. Clerk after clerk, Dick left a trail of lesser-than dolls in his wake. He didn't have many other gift ideas and he became anxious about possible failure.

∞∞

Just days before the implementation of Plan B – and there was no Plan B – there she was! Ballroom Barbie! He had heard Jane. He had acted. 'He-shoots-he scores!'

Encased in a clear plastic plinth, she/it was even dressed in a rich green ballgown that more or less matched the heavy brocade drapes that darkened their home. So far as he could recollect.

Dick was positively incandescent with anticipation. He was lit up by the internal flame of knowledge that his gift would resonate with his best intentions. As it turned out, however, instead of looking for Bionic Barbie, Dick should have been looking for Ironic Barbie. Same she/it in a very different wrapper.

∞∞

Christmas morning – his heart beating smugly, the large professionally wrapped gift radiating love and pride from beneath the burden of his romantic side – the time of unveiling finally arrived.

"You said you never had a Barbie!" Dick blurted out prematurely in excitement.

Jane paused as if in shock. She looked at Barbie. She looked at Dick. She looked at Barbie. Slowly, firmly, she finally expressed herself.

"Because I never wanted a f***ing Barbie," she pronounced indignantly. "You never listen!"

∞∞

Dick looks at her very differently now that it's just the two of them. He and Ballroom Barbie that is. He'd been head over heels at finding her. Now she is head over heels in a bin in the corner of their tiny apartment, next to the faded, brittle tinsel of that last Christmas, and the bloodied sword of dignity.

fin

JACK AND JILL
(TORRENTS AND TORMENTS)

"Don't fall!"

Jill always said that.

Are hers words of encouragement? Or a textbook redundancy. Like, 'try not to get hit by a bus,' or 'don't get shot.'

"Then don't push," Jack always teased in reply.

Stepping back from the brink of their latest conquest, Jack would dust off his hands in the time-honoured fashion and reach for their logbook.

"Bagged," he'd pronounce.

"Not yet. Take the picture," Jill always reminded.

"*Make* the picture," Jack always corrected.

∞∞

'Bagged' is a term adopted by diarizing hill-walkers in Scotland. To 'bag' a Munro, like bagging game on a hunt, is to have walked or climbed one of Scotland's many peaks of a certain elevation. Named for— well, you can Google that another time.

This story is about the figurative bagging of waterfalls. Jack and Jill's practice began ages ago during a Sunday outing that included Uisge Ban Falls, near Baddeck. The pounding, pulsing roar, the virility, the thundering torrent was somehow symbolic of the sensuality of a blossoming relationship.

Sometimes they bagged waterfalls on travels elsewhere in Canada and Scotland (which is where they got the idea to keep a record). They had swum naked in pools beneath the veils of broad falls, the cold waters failing to quench their passions. They'd made love beside remote rapids, their young bodies excited by the rocks smoothed by the ages and warmed by the sunshine.

At home, photographs of their children and families were interspersed with those of waterfalls, some of which likely had a role in the making of the children. Sometimes in the right evening light, the photos rekindled the rush of desire and passionate explorations.

∞∞

Over time, though, as happens to many – as they aged and as their children grew – the photos got dusty, and the journeys to the falls got fewer and more tedious. Their once-dizzying intimate explorations toward the climax of a cataract became less adventurous and of shorter duration – closer to the road, so to speak. Sometimes the hike proved too tedious altogether, and they couldn't get within reach of the falls. Neither could remember the last time they'd bagged a big one.

In time the kids left to follow their own trails, to find their own waterfalls. Patience for Jack and Jill's trips declined in proportion with patience for each other. At times Jack was taken aback that they had come to resemble one of those cranky old couples on television – funny and sad, not going anywhere, unable to resist occasional digs disguised as reminders or corrections in not-so-subtle undercurrents of sarcasm.

There was a deepening chasm of dry, dark and roiling emotions.

Neither kept score, but it was like they got some sort of satisfaction, a little emotional rush, out of their jagged barbs, taking pleasure in torments, not torrents. Where once they cuddled and coddled and delighted in the smallest of puddles, emotional rivers slowed to a trickle and all but dried up.

∞∞

In hopes it could be different, an anniversary trip to rekindle their passions was planned. A trip to bag the more remote North River Falls. Officially, the trail is closed – there would be fewer fellow hikers, if any.

Somehow, even in the normally sensuous presence of the impressive cataract, even as the concussion of the water pounded loudly on the jagged rocks below, it felt less like bliss and the depths of passion. It was more like the relentless drum of a pounding headache.

Undaunted, Jack took out the camera and edged closer to the precipice.

"Don't fall," Jill cautioned, again.

Jack turned awkwardly and, with a mischievous smirk, began his time-honoured retort, only to be brought up short by the look in Jill's eyes.

His reply was drowned out by the roar of the falls.

"Don't p—"

fin

STILL LIFE

Whether or not they acknowledge it, almost everyone wants to leave their mark on this world. Junior Mitton was one of those who tried. He really, really tried. This is his story. Stories, actually.

Junior Mitton would be eternally grateful for the attention paid to him by Henry, the elderly watchmaker in the shop next door. The old fellow always had time for him, Junior often punned.

Henry Odenthall's trade was clockmaker, but not many people needed clocks made or repaired anymore. Watchmaker was easier to say and remember. He was a damn fine cabinet maker too, specializing in handcrafted grandfather clocks and cuckoo clocks. But Junior and Henry's relationship was founded on their shared interest in photography. It was a hobby and a passion for both of them.

Henry's pictorial interests were in documentary photography, though he did not view it as anything so grand sounding as that. The walls of his repair shop displayed dozens of black-and-white photos of ordinary people going about their ordinary activities around the ordinary village that is The Landing. The naturally disordered depictions seemed in contrast with his very orderly and sparkling clean shop, where precision and a steady hand were requisite.

Right next door, Junior Mitton's stationery store and newsstand – ABC Stationery – displayed some of the photographs that Junior was most proud of. They were more on the artsy side. They shed light on the minutia of life around the area. Closeups, bold colours and strong lines were his way of revealing the extraordinary in the ordinary. In contrast with the sometimes surprisingly beautiful chaos revealed in his photographs, Junior's shop was neat and tidy, perhaps reflective of his generally quiet and orderly life.

The ABC in the shop's name also more or less reflected Junior's interests and personality – art and book, pictures and words. He found out fairly early that photography would never make him enough money to support himself, so he had added merchandise that made sense when put together.

Neither Junior nor Henry had any illusions about 'making it big' in The Landing or Cape Breton, and both were well-satisfied with their lot in life. Henry's singular service right next door was good for everyone's business. People often waited for their repairs, and often as not, spent time in other stores in the village, especially next door in ABC Stationery.

Junior and Henry often chatted about this. Actually, they chatted daily. Ever anxious for whatever business he could scrape together, Junior was in the practice of delivering the daily newspaper to subscribing businesses and shops along the road, including the clockmaker.

Junior always made an extra moment or two for Henry. They didn't always talk about their businesses but always talked about their shared interests – their art and their hopes for it. It's not like either really expected big things from it, but some recognition, some acknowledgement was nice when it came.

"Not likely," lamented Henry. He once related a story about art appreciation in Cape Breton.

This kind of thing happened more than once, apparently. As the only watch and clock repair service in Eastern Nova Scotia, Henry got a good many clients from distant towns and villages. Being right next door, Junior got a lot of benefit from the traffic to the old fellow's shop.

The story goes that two well-dressed women – who shall remain nameless – were in Henry's shop and took the time to admire some of the photographs on display.

"Greetings," they called out to Henry, who was behind the counter working on their repair job. Nodding to indicate the photographs, one woman remarked: "Great use of light. Look at the sparkle in that old man's eyes. It's just like they used to say: the photograph has captured his soul. And those hands! So full of strength and experience. And that one – such *lack* of emotion. What a good eye this photographer has – world-class."

At that point, as he told it, having completed his task, Henry came out from behind the counter and stood alongside the admirers as they continued to gush.

"Can you tell us who is this wonderful photographer? Where is he from?" asked one.

Henry puffed up a little and paused for dramatic effect before revealing that it was he, the clockmaker, and that he lived "right here in The Landing."

Well, you'd have thought they were caught admiring subliminal pornography. The photographs that moments before were world-class now were without class.

People are like that, Henry told Junior. People covet the famous. People respect the exotic and the rich. People dismiss the local.

There's an old story about a tourist strolling on a working wharf while fishermen were unloading their lobster catches. A bucket of very active lobsters drew the attention of the tourist, who called out to the fisherman that one of the lobsters was getting away. "Don't worry, ma'am," said the fisherman. "They're Cape Breton lobsters – if one gets too close to the top, the others will haul him back down."

The "B" in "ABC Stationery" was for books – previously loved books, mostly. Junior loved books. The store's inventory was largely his family's previously loved literature. Many of the books had occupied the store shelves for ages. Often that was because people would buy them, read them and return them for the benefit of future readers. People's patience with the process (paying for something, then giving it back without a refund) was a testament to the value they placed both in books and in the bookstore's survival.

It's not a bad business model when you think about it. Sell a book, then a few weeks later restock it to sell it again. Henry once gave Junior the bright idea to encourage readers to sign the books and to make notes in the margins. Some books were sporting an impressive provenance – a who's who of readers and admirers. Henry knew that there would be a certain cachet to certain titles if certain people indicated that they had read them. No doubt some names were under false pretences, but that could be just as entertaining as the book's contents. It did seem unlikely that someone named RL Stevenson read *The Strange Case of Dr. Jekyll and Mr. Hyde*, though entirely possible that someone named Peg Legge had read *Treasure Island.*

Junior loved books as much as he loved photography, and he hit upon an idea to combine the two, a collaboration with Henry. He'd always wanted to write a book, even though this one would be photographs and not many words. But, after all, every picture tells a story.

The idea was to juxtapose Henry's black-and-white photographs of selected local people and activities with Junior's contemporary colour versions. The idea had promise, they thought. Old alongside new. "The Landing, Then and Now," it was to be called.

Unfortunately, Henry Odenthall died of old age before anything could come of the idea.

∞∞

Henry Odenthall's death left holes in the life of The Landing, not the least of which was that left by the closure of Eastern Nova Scotia's only clock and watch repair shop. Though Junior was cognizant of the amount of business that Henry's shop brought into the village, he reasoned that the local population – aging and therefore diminishing though it was – appeared supportive of local businesses. With that support in mind, Junior expanded his premises by knocking out a wide doorway between the two stores.

He disposed of the counters and cabinets to create a small gallery, selling his photographs and Henry's side by side as he had intended for their book. Also on display – and more importantly for sale – was the work of local artists and artisans. The response to ABC Art and Stationery was immediate. It sparked so much local interest that Junior almost thought that people would buy stuff. They didn't. They mostly just looked.

So far as sales were concerned, business did not increase. In fact, it continued to decline – not precipitously but decline nonetheless. With a little more time on his hands after the renovations between customers, Junior's thoughts turned once more to his books – and, more importantly, to his dream of publishing a book of his own.

He just needed the right subject and the right push. His sister often urged that he just go ahead and do it. She suggested – that's a polite way of putting it – that all he had to do was publish a smutty novel, sell a million copies and *then* pursue something he considered worthwhile, whatever that was. It wouldn't matter if no one actually read it or understood it or even liked it. The point was to do it and move on. Junior insisted that he needed the right opportunity, so he waited.

He thought the wait was over when one quiet morning in the store he read a little-known fact about another of his elderly newspaper subscribers. The inspiration came from a throwaway line in a local history book that was long out of print. Mr. Franklin (Duckie) Dennis was a former peripheral politician, someone whose lifelong party affiliation was widely known and influential but whose aspirations did not include running for office. Most people regarded men like that as 'backroom boys.'

For two generations before Duckie the Dennis family was pretty deep in the coal mining business hereabouts. There is nothing really significant about that in and of itself because coal mining around here runs as deep in local families as the coal seams themselves run deep under the ocean.

What made the Dennis family's involvement seem extra special was the fact that one of their operations was the first underground mine to use a telephone to communicate with crews at the coal face. The telephone's predecessor, the telegraph, could not be used because of its sparks, but the telephone changed all that, improving not only communication but productivity and safety.

Duckie Dennis was a kind and generous friend. Apparently, he was the polar opposite of his father, but that's another story. Unlike his father, Duckie – as everyone knew him behind his back – was a man who never put on airs. He was equally attentive whether a person wore a blue collar, white collar, clerical collar or no collar.

Wealth is relative. Around here, the Dennis family was regarded as relatively wealthy. In his younger days – after his notoriously critical father had passed away – Duckie and his wife were world travellers. Once achieving the status of 'elderly,' the then-retired businessman and heir managed his money and studied history from his small, rented office on the second floor of the former bank building.

Duckie was a Rotarian. He enjoyed the association with others afforded by the Rotary Club, the members of which were, for the most part, well-heeled, well educated, worldly and, more importantly, generous and empathetic citizens. The club was perfect for Duckie, and he for it. The group offered him ample and continuous opportunities for both camaraderie and community service.

Duckie was also an amateur photographer. He had more gear and gadgets in his office and in the attic of his home than many shops – including Junior Mitton's collection. Through their shared interest, Duckie and Junior became close friends. Whenever the former was cleaning his office in town or the attic at home, he would come across some forgotten piece of equipment or accessory and, on account of his advanced age, gift it to Junior. Everything from musty camera bags to telephoto lenses to slide trays to antique cameras became curiosities and conversation pieces in ABC Art and Stationery.

One summer evening, Junior got a phone call inviting him to the office – Duckie wanted to discuss a certain matter with him. Junior didn't need to be coaxed. Attending to the second-floor sanctum, he found Duckie examining an old photo album. A bottle of their favourite single-malt whisky and two respectable-size whisky glasses were at his elbow. The album was a pictorial record of his family's yacht – a vintage cabin cruiser with an impressive history, including having been commandeered by the navy during the war.

Accustomed to years of Duckie's generosity (antique cameras and the like), Junior thought to himself, 'Oh my God. Is he going to give me his yacht!?'

Duckie turned a page in the album. The yacht was being sold to a prominent New Brunswick family.

'Get a grip,' Junior chided himself. 'Give your head a shake,' as they say in Newfoundland. 'Stupid. Stupid.'

Duckie then pointed out several photographs of fine china that had been commissioned by one of the yacht's previous owners – perhaps the original owner.

'Oh my God,' thought Junior, looking sidelong at the whisky and the still-empty glasses, 'he knows I sometimes buy old china at auctions. Is he giving me the china?'

Duckie explained that he planned to sell the china to the yacht's new owners.

'Stupid. Stupid. Stupid,' Junior repeated to himself. He felt flushed and longed to reach for that whisky.

Duckie then asked Junior what he thought about the sale of the china; the proceeds would go to the Rotary Club as a donation. "What do you think?"

"Of course," Junior gushed. He was starting to sweat from embarrassment. 'Stupid. Selfish. Stupid.'

The real reason Junior tells this story has only a loose connection with the yacht and its china. It has more to do with mining, photography and, of course, books.

The more time Junior spent with Duckie, the more he learned about him and his family's history. Why not connect that with local history? In a way, the Dennis family history was the history of the whole area – personal, political and professional. They'd title it "Deep Roots," a play on underground mines and family trees.

Such a story could be presented parallel with historical events in the local area. A detailed historical narrative could be created around the Dennis family over the generations – their businesses, especially mining, their travels, etc. It would add a lot of local colour to an account of generations – or vice versa. Junior planned to discuss it with Duckie and his wife, but he had to wait for the right moment.

Before they could hammer out the details, however, Franklin (Duckie) Dennis died.

∞∞

Junior incorporated many of his late friend's photographic artifacts in his gallery – he did not include any artifacts or photos of the Dennis's yacht.

It's hard when someone you love or admire is at death's door. It can also be difficult to know when death is imminent, whether it's a loved one, or a beloved pet or even a home. On some level, grounds for grief also apply to supposedly less personal things – like a village. Those were the thoughts that vexed Junior Mitton when he had too much time on his hands, and he had plenty of that.

Junior's feelings of foreboding were at their height as he renovated ABC (now ABC News and Views) yet again. This time it was a reverse renovation. He closed off the passage he had opened up just a few years before because the volume of traffic through his shop reflected that of the village: slow. General outmigration diminished the local population and, in turn, services and so on. The writing was on the wall, and the walls seemed to be closing in.

There were stalwarts of stability among local residents, of course, but they were fewer. One of the stalwarts was Captain Georges Detcheverry. Cap'n Georgie, as he was known around The Landing, was a daily visitor who preferred to pick up his paper in person. He liked to walk to the village for his newspapers (Junior also ordered in the French paper specially for him), chat a little and then go for coffee at The Miller's Oven, where he would read the papers before heading home again.

Cap'n Georgie (Georges was just too hard for people to get their tongues around, likewise Detcheverry) was a well-known mariner with a half-century of experience in the North Atlantic. A native of the French islands of Saint-Pierre-et-Miquelon, he had retired to The Landing to be nearer his wife's family (the MacInnises). The village, on the shore of Loch Bras d'Or, was about as much salt water and marine weather as he wanted in retirement.

The Detcheverrys lived in a solid-looking wooden house firmly anchored to a ridge overlooking the village, yet sheltered from the marine weather. Their home sported a deck and railing on two sides where Cap'n

Georgie paced several times a day as though inspecting the village below for seaworthiness.

He was full of stories about his years on the water, stories he liked to share with anyone who showed genuine interest. Every day, Junior was that audience, but one story in particular detailed a voyage that seemed doomed. It was a story that Junior would never forget.

Cap'n Georgie and his crew were aboard a medium-size freighter that is typical of the area, plying the waters of the Gulf of St. Lawrence between Quebec and wherever, when one of those "once-in-a-hundred-years" storms overtook them. The Gulf is not particularly deep – not that it's particularly shallow – and that day, the sea rose to such great heights that the corresponding troughs were extraordinarily deep. As deep as any of them had ever experienced.

Recollection of that particular voyage was something you might read in Jules Verne or Edgar Alan Poe, or both. Crest after crest, great foaming mountains of frigid sea tossed their ship into the sky, only to suck it down the mountains in the troughs between. As though on some demonic rollercoaster ride, they rose and rose, only to dive and dive, and dive some more. Incredibly, they felt the ship touch the bottom. They touched the bottom!

Cap'n Georgie felt it. The ship's mate felt it. They all must have felt it and felt the terrifying shudder of the ship's steel structures before almost immediately nosing upward on the next wave. Up they went with a nauseating reversal of gravity in near-total darkness, the lights of the ship were consumed by the disorienting darkness that engulfed them.

All aboard counted the sea's undulations as they fairly flew down and then up the next series of waves.

Each man dreaded the inevitability of the seventh and largest wave in each series. Each man held on for dear life as they counted, their grips tightening as they did. All eyes were raised toward the heavens above each rise and lowered toward hell on each dive.

Again they hit bottom, this time with the devastating effect of loss of power. No power meant what little control they had under the circumstances was extinguished along with their lights. In complete darkness, the ship's climb out of the trough was now more of a wriggle, its gyrations felt as shudders, as though the ship sensed the seemingly inevitable outcome of their peril.

Imagine the shock to one's system. Think of the heart-sinking feeling knowing you have struck that bottomless bottom and knowing further that, towering overhead, the next colossus was advancing to fill the airspace above you. Small comfort that the ship did not rest on the bottom with any finality. The keel struck, but immediately they rose on the next wave into the darkness above them. No lights. No navigation other than a worn compass that was normally ignored in favour of electronics. No engines meant no rudder. No communication meant no help. No hope.

It is no secret that a great many mariners are believers – believers in God, that is, or in a higher power at least. When imminent death is a constant in your life, it must be comforting to believe in a divinity. Of the benevolent sort, one would think.

As skipper, Cap'n Georgie knew that the ship and their lives were in jeopardy, and each man aboard knew it too. When all you can do is ride it out, the only other thing you can do is pray. According to Cap'n Georgie, pray they did. Each time the ship raced down the next wave, they prayed.

Junior didn't recall how long Cap'n Georgie said that the ordeal continued – once would be enough for most people. Obviously, the story had a satisfactory ending because he lived to tell it. They did not hit bottom a third time, but that is not the end of the story, and it was the ending that struck Junior Mitton.

As the ship crested the seventh of the next series of waves – beyond which another deep and threatening trough waited like a submarine monster, a leviathan – the crew saw light piercing the dark at a distance. Only it wasn't a light; it was the moon shining through an opening in the clouds, an opening just big enough to allow it and a little hope to shine through.

The moon was soon extinguished by the next seventh wave, one so monstrous that *all* light was extinguished. This one would surely sink them. While the other crewmembers tightened their grips on anything solid, each gazed heavenward, perhaps in hope of glimpsing the moon again, in part perhaps to prepare for the end. Cap'n Georgie's eyes were transfixed by his compass readings.

He didn't need a compass to know of their peril. He knew these waters. He knew where they were. He understood what awaited them in their helpless state: certain death.

What he couldn't understand were the mixed messages he was getting from his compass. They should have hit bottom again because they were getting closer to the shore. Still some distance off in the dark were jagged cliffs, the outcropping of the upward-sloping seabed, and those cliffs were dead ahead. Dead ahead – how often we use that phrase without considering its sinister implications.

Wide-eyed, Cap'n Georgie remained transfixed by the compass. When the ship and its terrified crew crested the next wave, the compass and the ship were pointing in a different heading: they were pointed toward home. When they crested the next wave, the moon was fully visible. The clouds parted, and the sea was less violent. Each subsequent crest brought new hope. Before long, the storm had all but passed, and the crew began to scramble, each to their assigned tasks under such well-rehearsed circumstances.

Illuminated only by their battery-powered torches, some working feverishly below decks to clear the mess, the chief engineer worked to resuscitate the engine and, therefore, the ship's power and mobility. In the darkness the rest of the crew busied themselves in anticipation and faith in their mates below.

Cap'n Georgie continued to watch in amazement and confusion as the skies continued to clear and the seas continued to calm. The stars and the moon shone brightly. The compass showed which way was home and safety, and the rudderless ship somehow steered them accordingly. With a shake of his head, Cap'n Georgie tried to clear his mind to the various tasks at hand, tasks he knew so well in principle but were seldom called upon.

Just as the St. Paul's Island light made itself known, the ship's engines roared to life. Power restored and systems seemingly unaffected, the helm responded to Cap'n Georgie's instructions. With only minor adjustment, he pointed the ship toward home.

Lost in their thoughts, feeling safe in the throaty rumble of the engines and the occasional squawk of the radio, the crew restored order from chaos, precious life from certain death.

It was an astonishing story by any stretch of the imagination and of any creed. It came to Junior that there were likely many similar stories to be collected, not only from Cap'n Georgie but from the many mariners in the local area as well. There might or might not be photographs available to complement such stories, but maybe he could replicate their mood artistically.

He even came up with a title for the book: "Fury, Fear, and Fate: Divine Intervention on the High Seas." Anyone he spoke with about the idea thought it would make a fine book. Chuffed about the prospect, Junior knew he had to start with Cap'n Georgie's stories. Together they would come up with a plan.

By the time he got around to approaching him, however, Captain Georges Detcheverry had died.

∞∞

You wouldn't say that he was despondent over the death of the elderly mariner – nor of his other old friends – but Junior was very aware of the coincidences. Three false starts and three deaths: Was the universe trying to tell him something?

That his shop was slowly turning into a mausoleum was brought home by the addition of marine artifacts given to him by Cap'n Georgie's widow. Junior thought it was getting a bit crowded. Because local people frequently directed visitors to his curiosities, he hoped that selling coffee, tea and locally sourced baked goods might rejuvenate his business. He hadn't referred to it as a real business in years.

By serving coffee, activity in the little shop was indeed revived, in a manner of speaking. Opening hours were extended, and locals stopped by more often, sharing coffee, conversation and stories, and occasionally even making other purchases.

It took a few years to recognize, but without a critical mass of the kinds of services vital to village life, its lifeblood, so to speak, The Landing seemed to be slowly dying. Junior wondered if ABC Arts and Artifacts was also doomed. On more than one occasion, over a couple of drinks, mind you, Junior's closest associates quipped that he might consider making a business out of his bad luck. "Fortune from failure," joked one. "Have Pen, Will Travel," suggested another. Joking aside, it was high time to get serious.

Junior Mitton had never before considered himself a failure, per se, but he was beginning to think that way, just as things were beginning to look that way in The Landing in general. Young people were moving away, businesses were shuttered, and tourism was practically non-existent. It all made for a level of pessimism.

When he felt like that – when he felt as though failure was imminent, especially at the end of most months – Junior poured himself a cup of unsold coffee and got down one of the store's well-worn copies of *Chicken Soup for the Soul.* He knew most of the stories by heart by now but longed to find some magic thought that might help turn things around – or give him a good idea for a book, of course. It lifted his spirits somewhat just to read those inspiring 'can-do' anecdotes.

Junior still got ideas for books all the time, but the successive failures had been off-putting to say the least. All he had to show for his ambitions were a few photographs on the walls, notebooks full of ideas, descriptions and quotes from people who no longer spoke for themselves. He felt that his book ideas always came to him too late or that he took too long to write down those stories. How to turn them into chicken soup, that was the question.

The demise of ABSea Books and Crafts, as it was now called, became a certainty. It was just a matter of time. That he knew. He was either a poor businessperson or the dying village had such a small population and so few tourists that it could no longer support his efforts. The inventory of toys, books, photographs and artifacts was more like a museum than a business.

He wasn't getting any younger, and he had yet to find out if he was even a decent photographer, let alone a passable writer. He continued to think that the only real test of his abilities, the only real way to leave his mark on the world, was in the publication of something he had created.

But in contemplating what he saw as a litany of bad luck, a grain of an idea sprouted. He knew what he had to do. Stories. Not just one story. That was his purpose. That would be his book.

Junior set out to capitalize not only on his obvious passions but the passions of others. On their many stories. "Their Stories, Our History" was born. Well, it was conceived.

The Landing was his muse. He would listen to anyone with a good story to tell and add their tales to his collection. He would keep his fingers crossed that they'd get the whole story out before they died. But if they did die, which seemed likely since The Landing was largely comprised of old-timers anyway, it would be a way for their families to remember them and to add their story to an accumulating history.

∞∞

The stationery, book, art, crafts, toys, souvenirs, pseudo museum and coffee shop got seedier over time. Well-used books occupied floor-to-ceiling shelves, tastefully interspersed with deeply discounted toys, photographs and old cameras. The occasional tourist admired and sometimes even bought a photograph or two. Junior devoted less and less time to the store and more and more time to gathering the lives of The Landing in stories and photographs into neatly labelled boxes at the back of the store.

We've renamed the old store. It's Mitton's now – just Mitton's. Junior's treasured boxes remain where they were left at the back, their contents waiting for the right moment, for the right person. Maybe we'll get around to finishing the book someday, but we're new to The Landing; there will be plenty of time for that.

fin

THE PRICE OF BROCCOLI

"I wonder if she moved away? We haven't seen her car there in ages."

"I haven't seen any other cars there lately, either. Maybe she's finally moved to the home."

"Forced to give up her independence. Too bad."

"Maybe she finally gave up the car. A car's not cheap. She can take a taxi for supplies and back three times a week for what a car costs."

"With money left over for a trip to Disney."

"She's tough. We've got to give her that. There's never a thing out of place."

"Except the weeds."

"I think the weeds are intentional. No lawn to speak of. No grass to mow. Just a few patches."

"Lots of patches on her trailer."

"It must be more than sixty years old."

"Older, I think. They say it was moved up here when the trailer court closed after the heavy water plant shut. That was more than forty years ago."

"That big patch on the corner of it has been there as long as I can remember."

"More duct tape than aluminum."

"A new patch or two every year, and that one gets bigger. It's a wonder that place holds any heat."

"Was she there last winter? I don't remember. Maybe she moves in with family in the winters."

"No woodpile. Must be expensive to heat that thing."

"A wood burner isn't safe in a trailer."

"They don't call them trailers anymore. Too trashy. Minihomes sounds better."

"She can afford getting the newspaper delivered every day."

"No dish for Internet or for television – unless it's on the back."

"We'd all be better off without that stuff anyway. A tea kettle and a library card are all a person needs."

"We rarely see a light. Not that we drive much at night."

"I don't like driving at night anymore – or in the rain."

"You're getting old."

"You're keeping up."

"So is everyone else around here. If it wasn't for church, bingo and chance meetings at the grocery store you'd think every house was empty."

"There are cars in most yards."

"They hardly leave the yards except for church and on cheque day."

"Cheques don't go far."

∞∞

"Geez. That was like going to a wake."

"What?"

"The grocery store. It's the same every week. People paying their respects to the meat cooler. Walking by slowly, sadly, stooping and squinting at the prices. Shaking their heads in disbelief. Like they're reading the cards on funeral flowers."

"Ha! Right. A distant smile. Recollection of a time when meat was a part of our lives."

"Can't afford the vegetables, for that matter. Even when they are on sale. Half the time the lettuce is brown, and so is the cauliflower. The broccoli's so old it's gone to seed. That must be why they charge double."

"What the heck do you do with Swiss chard?"

"Maybe free trade with Europe will mean we can afford cheeses again."

"And Belgian chocolate."

"And sausages."

"And premium Italian paper."

"There are a few clothes drying on her line today."

"Well worn. That red sweater has seen better days."

"Why would she install those driveway markers if she doesn't have a car?"

"Precisely spaced. That must have taken her a day or two."

"Or whoever helps her, I suppose. She wouldn't need them if she didn't have a car."

"Exactly the same height, precisely spaced, brand new reflective tape. She's tough, I'll give her that."

"You have to admire that she manages all alone."

"Surely family members look in on her – help her with some things."

"Probably. Families are close around here."

"Do you mind if I stop in for a haircut while we're in town?"

"Drop me at the mall, then, and meet me when you're done."

∞∞

"There are two newspapers on the driveway this morning. Obviously she didn't get down to the road yesterday."

"It's been raining."

"Not yesterday."

"True."

"She has to be careful not to go out too early. There was another cougar sighting last week."

"I don't know whether to believe that or not."

"Who to believe? Wildlife officers say absolutely no cougars around here. Locals see them – one at least – fairly regular."

"So, what's on the list today?"

"If we are going for coffee, let's do that first – before groceries – because we need milk and eggs."

"And meat. And I want to go to the hardware store."

"Again?"

"I want to price paint for the bedroom."

"Just don't ask me what colour."

"Or for your help. Don't worry I won't."

"You know I'm poor at painting."

"So you would have me believe."

"Her porch could do with some new paint."

∞∞

"Is that the mobile? Reception kicks in around here. Right by her trailer."

"Shit, I forgot about it."

"Is it in your purse?"

"Missed call. It was Francis."

"Call him back, would you? I told him to call if he needed anything from town. He has a cold."

"That's what neighbours are for. He's not getting any younger."

"We're invited over for tea later. We'll have to pick up something to bring."

"As long as we're home in time for *Ellen*."

∞∞

"Watch out!"

"Jesus! That pothole gets bigger every week."

"Sinkhole, more like it."

"It's a good thing there was nothing coming, and no tourists on the road at this hour."

"I'm going to have to call the Highways again and complain – again. Someone's going to lose a wheel."

"I hear that the school bus driver has to wear a kidney belt."

"I heard she broke another axle on that bus. Three in three years. Not safe for the little ones."

"The curtains are still closed."

"Against the cold, maybe. Windows are frosted up."

"There's a light on in the kitchen; you can see where the curtains are thin."

"How do you know it's the kitchen?"

"All trailers had the same layout for years."

"It's bright enough today. She wouldn't need a light on if the curtains were open. It's not like she can afford it, I wouldn't think."

"Probably too exposed to leave them open. She might feel vulnerable with them open."

∞∞

"She'll have to watch it on the ice today. Can't risk a fall at her age."

"How old did you say?"

"I didn't. I don't know. Eighties, maybe?"

"Likely."

"Did someone keep her driveway cleared last winter? I don't remember."

"She doesn't need it plowed if she doesn't drive."

"It still needs to be cleared. Someone must drive her up to the door. Or take her groceries up."

"True. It's just the first snow, anyway. It will be gone in a couple of days."

"I think we should have our driveway paved."

"It's too expensive, isn't it? Asphalt or concrete?"

"I'm not sure. I think concrete is more expensive, but lasts longer. Either would make snow removal easier."

"I heard ice forms more readily on concrete, which means more salt, and that's not good for it. Asphalt is best, I think."

"Maybe we should ask around, see if any of the neighbours are thinking the same."

"Try to get a better price."

"Do you have the list? Where to first?"

"We need meat if there's any left. And eggs. So, groceries last. Go for coffee first?"

"Sure. And maybe a treat?"

∞∞

"I wish you'd slow down. It might be icy under the snow."

"They are damned slow getting the highway snow plow out this morning."

"I thought I heard it during the night."

"It looks like they laid down some salt before the snow started. It snowed more than was forecast. They should have come around again by now."

"I don't know why we need to go to town this early, anyway. We could have waited until later – until it's properly plowed."

"It's cheque day. If we don't get ahead of the crowd there won't be any fresh vegetables left worth buying."

"Slow down for the turn."

"Lots of traffic at her place earlier this morning, by the look of things. Between snowfalls I'd say."

"Geez, no-one for months and now the whole town visits."

"At least one of them should have cleared some snow away instead of driving right through it. When that freezes, no one is getting in or out. No brains in some people."

"And there is a mess of snow still on her steps. They just walked right through it! She'll fall and break her hip one of these days, mark my words."

"It's not like her to let that go. She always keeps the steps clear."

"I wonder if she'll move away from all the work. Maybe into a home. It's too much for an old woman."

"Not by the look of the traffic this morning."

"Maybe she's finally moving in with family for the winter."

"Another year or two and she'll have to. Does she have any family? Maybe into a home if she can afford it. Even if it's is just for the winters."

"That would make sense. At least someone would be looking out for her."

"Should we go for coffee?"

fin

MRS. COFFEY'S OPUS

At the ripe age of eighty-eight, Mrs. Coffey could still recognize the child in every adult she met, even if they hadn't lived in the village since leaving school.

Mrs. Coffey, as everyone will forever know her, was the teacher in the local school for decades – "since Christ were a cowboy," Phonsie Sampson once said. Phonsie moved to The Landing as a boy, but his Acadian upbringing, accent and wicked sense of humour added a little whimsy to the nearly homogeneous, often dour and sober Scots sensibilities predominant hereabouts.

Having so much influence over so many impressionable young minds, Euphemia Coffey was The Landing's moral compass. That's not because of her grandmotherly appearance but because of her penchant for discipline. She expected, and for the most part received, respect for rules and rote. Two generations of males in these parts bear the imprint of Mrs. Coffey's well-worn mathematics textbook in response to foolishness, bad behaviour or being too thick-headed for even basic math.

She had greater expectations of girls because she didn't have to whack them; girls never seemed to act up in class or in the yard.

The boys referred to her as "Perk" when out of earshot – combining the obvious with the fact that her temper, when someone dared to test the water, could be scalding. Over a half century, everyone who called The Landing home was corrected by her heavy hand and quick, firm opinions "since time immoral," Phonsie said.

As a teacher and as a pillar of the community, Mrs. Coffey's word was sacrosanct and as such she was expected to uphold its conservative values. In light of that, she caused raised eyebrows when she got a television, the first person in the parish to do so.

It was a turning point that turned heads in our village at the time – "and some 'eads clear 'round," according to Phonsie – something that all of a certain generation recall about her. In our present condition, the equivalent might be the first person to NOT have a television.

In a double standard not obvious to adolescent school boys, Mrs. Coffey instantly became pretty cool for her age as far as we kids were concerned. Most older people, mostly un-cool, were wary of "the idiot box," a reference to the fact that some people, particularly impressionable children, are apparently drawn to merely sit and stare at it for prolonged periods. They should be out chopping wood, or cleaning out the stalls, or plucking chickens, or memorizing the Bible.

I sometimes wondered if grown-ups feared television would expose their children – themselves, even – to things beyond the loch and the forest that darkened it. "A sma' window to a big world," Phonsie once said in a flash of thoughtfulness.

Surely Mrs. Coffey's blessing was a signal that watching TV would not, in fact, rot your brains, as was so often and so vehemently proselytized by my Presbyterian grandmothers – yes, both of them. That was, of course, a pretty favourable endorsement of TV and Mrs. Coffey as far as I was concerned. Many a rainy day after school and all summer long, Mrs. Coffey's book-lined parlour would have a half-dozen barefoot waifs, too young for chores at home, supping milk and cookies while glued to whatever was on TV.

Even in retirement she had rules. Just because she was no longer the real school teacher didn't mean children could let up on their schoolwork. Or so she said. I don't know if anyone tested her.

Book learning wasn't foremost in people's minds in the old days – what with being hungry and cold – but when the electrics finally reached almost everyone, and with it TV, it kind of opened up the world to all kinds of things.

These days we still don't have much good to say about television in general – maybe grandma was right about it – but like I said, back then it really opened people's eyes. Mrs. Coffey saw the writing on the wall, so to speak, and she did her utmost to prepare us for the wider world we discovered was 'out there.' You don't have to be literary to be literate.

TV came rather late to our village for the simple reason that electricity was rather late coming to our village. For reasons I couldn't follow back then, that was blamed on the lack of decent roads. Then, things seemed to come all at once – better roads brought more cars, electricity followed, then refrigerators and televisions.

If you expressed even passing interest in something you saw on the TV or in a book on her wall, she was quick to encourage you to learn more about it. She'd even lend out a book, like her parlour was a library. You didn't even have to promise to read it, just to treat it with respect and to return it in good condition. I certainly abided by those rules and suppose most did, at the very least to ensure there would be future sessions in front of her television. Some may even have read a few books.

In retirement she couldn't use school work or grades as a stick – or whack us with one – but she had an air of authority about her that kept us mindful; if she couldn't control a classroom, she was in complete control of the television.

In retrospect, the barrage of communications may have been the beginning of the end for The Landing and other rural communities like it. Plenty of people say it was the Canso Causeway that started the exodus, but I say it was TV. Mind you, it wasn't the start of the decline; that credit goes to the wars. And the Liberals.

Mrs. Coffey wasn't from around here directly – she was from St. George's Channel – but her late mother was from here – a double MacLeod; their people were from Skye, I think – and for sure she had that Highland stubborn streak coursing through her veins.

I sort of remember her husband. He too came from across the loch, but that's not why most children were afraid of him. He had been in the war. At first he seemed alright, unlike old man McGillivray, for whom the term "dead drunk" might be credited.

As a returned veteran, it wasn't too long before Mr. Coffey got a job at one of the local quarries, but he lasted only one day. The story goes that when they set off the first charge of dynamite on his first day, the explosion caused him to drop to the ground, hollering and covering his head like a child in a nightmare. After that, he spent his days on their front veranda, sitting very still and wild-eyed, just watching the world go by. No one let on there was anything wrong with him – respecting his status as a veteran, tossing him a wave or a nod as they hurried by.

Phonsie remarked to me once that going into the old teacher's house after school must have been like "goin' to Grammar's 'ouse," complete with the big bad wolf at the door. In the evenings, you could see him through the parlour window, staring emotionless at the television. Maybe she got it for him.

He spent almost twenty years like that. He died just as quietly as he lived. All the grown-ups were sympathetic, but to tell the truth, he'd for so long been a silent witness to life in The Landing that it was like he was already dead.

Mrs. Coffey had been allowed to keep on teaching. Normally a woman had to quit once she got married, but his being away at the war, and later his infirmity and his death meant that she was kept on. She taught for many more years until the house was paid for, then she got by on the veteran's widow pension and the generosity of neighbours. Neighbours like Iain Dubh.

For a time, some folks thought she'd hooked up with Iain Dubh, an older bachelor and former student of hers from 'back the glen.' He helped her with repairs and keeping up the yard. He came and went fairly regular, more regular than one would expect for such a little yard. Phonsie saw a contradiction in his service – Iain Dubh had quit school at a young age and could hardly read or write, yet the teacher couldn't get by without him.

Regardless of his practical example of utility, parents warned their kids that they had to get an education or they would end up like Iain Dubh, instead of like Mrs. Coffey. Their relationship was doubly ironic, given their relations when Iain Dubh was still in school. Indeed, many blamed Perk for his having quit.

∞∞

Iain Dubh had a wicked stutter. Curiously, he stuttered in the English but not in the Gaelic, his mother's tongue. Try as she might, Mrs. Coffey couldn't cure him, either by "'ook 'er by book," Phonsie might say. She didn't coddle him, but she did go easy on him when it came time for class participation and oral reading skills and the like. There was enough of the Gaelic around in those days that he got by just fine outside the classroom. Mrs. Coffey didn't have the Gaelic.

The story goes that when he was ten or twelve, a new family moved into the area. The man was a Mountie. The woman stayed at home like most moms did in those days, and their two kids went to the school in The Landing. The younger fellow was nice enough, but the older one was a bit of a bully. He had something to say about everything and everyone, but he was merciless when it came to anyone speaking Gaelic – as most did from time to time. And he was at his meanest when it came to Iain Dubh's stutter.

One day, his last day of school as it turned out, Iain Dubh had enough, and when Lionel, the Mountie's son, brushed by him in obvious belligerence, Iain Dubh decked him. Lionel found his feet quick enough, and as he stood, he grabbed Iain Dudh at the waist, lifting him clean off his feet; the pair of them ended up rolling around on the ground in a tight but violent embrace. Whoever was on top in a given moment was the one delivering the beating.

Mrs. Coffey weighed in after Lionel's little brother ran inside to tell her that Iain Dubh was killing Lionel. Mrs. Coffey came across the yard in a flash, just as Iain Dubh was sensing victory and getting to his feet out of the way of Lionel's flailing arms and legs. She grabbed Iain Dubh from behind with such force he was driven once more to his knees.

He was up again as quick as a flash, right fist loaded to launch at the as-yet-unseen assailant. When he turned and saw just who was responsible, he froze, fist still positioned for retaliation. Legend has it that Mrs. Coffey motioned with both hands outstretched, palms up, wiggling her fingers and daring him in the time-honoured tradition of 'you-want-a-piece-of-me?'

Behind him, Lionel got to his feet. Rather than let things go, Lionel put his hands on his hips, leaned forward, and mocked his opponent, "be-be-beat by a o-ol-old lady!" Ignoring him, Iain Dubh dropped his fists and his shoulders in defeat, strode across the yard, and through the schoolhouse door. He re-emerged after only a moment with his jacket, cap and books. Handing the books to Mrs. Coffey, he turned and headed up the path toward his home. He never returned to school.

∞∞

Anyway, the elders did slowly get used to the whole TV thing. I suppose that gradually other households started to have them and, pressured by their children, had little reason to mutter criticism of TV if Mrs. Coffey had one. What really scandalized everyone for the longest time, though, was the sight of grown men coming away from her door at all hours. And not just Iain Dubh.

Over the years, there was plenty of tongue-wagging and knowing chin-pointing when fellows my father's age and older were seen leaving with smiles on their faces and colour in their cheeks. I wasn't privy to the adult conversations on the church steps after services, but I sensed that she was a target from time to time. Still, it was Mrs. Coffey, and the scandal was addressed only when she was out of earshot.

I know what you're thinking because the visits were mostly after dark – though, in fairness, there's only about eight hours of daylight around here half the year. The visits didn't happen during school hours, or when we children were watching her TV, so it all seemed very grown-up and hush-hush. Later in life, I learned that when there are gaps in people's understandings, their tongues fill those gaps, and it's usually has a bitter taste.

So too when it comes to teachers, a lot of people seem to hold a grudge for a long, long time. Some get over it or at least keep their criticisms to themselves when their own kids have to get along with teachers. Some, unfortunately, tend to poison the next generation against teachers and schools in general. Still others can be forgiven if the system, or the teacher, treated them badly.

I don't mean to imply that the younger generation was oblivious to the adult nods and hushed recriminations. Kids know a lot more than adults want them to – or give them credit for. If there was something going on between Mrs. Coffey and a few of the old-timers in our little cove, we didn't let on for fear of being overheard – for fear of losing our TV privileges.

It was an incentive to keep up with our schoolwork and keep down with the questions. Some of us were partial to the series-type shows, and we'd do everything we could to be in front of the box at certain times on certain days.

For some reason, my childhood recollections of television programming differ from the recollections of others my age. Memories of the hours spent in Mrs. Coffey's parlour are a curious amalgam of our collective youth. I say "our" because I've discussed this with some of my peers, and though we have similar recollections, they are not identical.

One of the favourite shows of my youth was *Forest Rangers*, which portrayed a youthful troop of environmentalists – though I never heard that word until decades later. I recall them solving mysteries and rescuing small animals. I miss shows like that.

I'm pretty sure I recall correctly that programming in those days began only after school, after 3 p.m. or thereabouts, except on weekends. I also remember endless episodes of *Roy Rogers, The Lone Ranger,* and *Chez Hélène,* but my peers tell me that these were not necessarily broadcast in the same years or even in the same decade, so they may not actually be recollections of afternoons at Mrs. Coffey's.

Still, it says something about my youthful memories being centred, as they were, around TV and, therefore, Mrs. Coffey. It was years before I connected my working life as a landscaper with the hours spent watching *Forest Rangers* in Mrs. Coffey's living room. "She kep' you well grounded," Phonsie punned more than once.

Two of my favourite books from those early reading days came from Perk's library – *The Adventures of Tom Sawyer, The Adventures of Huckleberry Finn* and *Here Stays Good Yorkshire.* Okay, that's three books, but the two Mark Twain books are like one long one. Believe it or not, I can still quote from them, along with some Shakespeare that she made us read in school.

A positive thing I do remember from her lessons, and her parlour, was that she sometimes told us *why* we needed to know stuff, you know? People I have worked with or drank with over the years regretted that they'd had little respect for school because they couldn't see the sense of it. When you're out in the work world, sometimes you reflect on how you got there and how things might have been different.

Phonsie Sampson never quite got it. He couldn't figure out the relevance of the "'den-to-now" relationship between history books and present-day life. Why, he asked, did he need to look at pictures of naked Greeks on dishes – obviously painted on cold days, if you catch his meaning. He was destined to become a fisherman like his father and his father's father. For me, sometimes studying about multiple Greek gods and godesses was not all that helpful when I was busy worshipping the teenage goddesses all around me – and picturing them painted on dishes.

I never went to college but I think I could have if Mrs. Coffey had gotten her way. She came to see my parents one time, to tell them that I could probably go to college because I was smart enough. I can still recall that visit. Whenever company came, the dogs heard them coming up the road and gave a noisy warning so that we kids could race to the house to see who got to wear the shoes.

My parents weren't too fussy about the college idea. They said if I was smart enough, I was smart enough. They said that if I went away to college, I'd just keep on going, and I was needed on the farm like my father was, and like his father too.

They were right, of course. I didn't want to go to college or even to consider it, but it was nice of her to say so. I was hot-to-trot off that mud patch we called a farm and to start making a living. My uncle Dougie got me a job in the steel plant in Hamilton before I moved to Toronto.

I credit Mrs. Coffey's TV for making me realize there is more to the world than The Landing and Port Hawkesbury. It wasn't her fault that, later, I couldn't see going backward from Toronto or that after a night at the tavern singing "Farewell to Nova Scotia" and "Out on the Mira." I sometimes wished I was back there for more than old home week and every other Christmas.

∞∞

Anyway, here we are, the whole damned village and most everyone who ever lived here and was still "among the quick," like the Bible says. Or maybe that was Shakespeare. Mrs. Coffey had the decency to die during old home week, when every room, sofa and cot in every house was occupied with family from across the island and across the country. Every yard, field and gravel pit had a tent or trailer parked on it. It was the same every summer.

She'd dropped dead at her kitchen table without finishing her supper. "Dined wit' 'er boots on," Phonsie punned. No illness, no hospital time, no wringing of hands. Gone. Here one day, not the next. On. Off.

She was waked in the well-kept old house where she had lived for about sixty years and where two generations – and maybe a few from a third – were schooled in the-ways-of-the-world-according-to-Mrs. Coffey.

The line of people paying their respects spilled out of her front door, down the drive and up the road. I know for a fact that among them were those who had said bad things about her while she was alive, but we're nothing if not bound by ceremony – we of Highland descent. You wouldn't miss such an event because people would notice you missed it. And you never know, reckoned Phonsie, she was probably up in heaven taking attendance.

It was kind of awkward for everyone that Mrs. Coffey didn't have any family to sit up with her, or to greet people at the door, or to put out a lunch in the usual way. The ladies from the kirk stepped up and took care of some of those things. With no one to guide funeral and disposal arrangements, the lady minister from the English church across the road kindly took charge of those things. Iain Dubh, Phonsie and I sat up with her one night, well-fortified against the spectre of ghosts raised by the stories we shared.

The service was to be held in the community hall. That was fitting because it was once the school – Mrs. Coffey's school. What few children there are now get bused to a school an hour away. Using the hall meant having one of those electric pianos instead of the church organ, though, and that set some tongues wagging. But Mrs. Campbell, the choir leader from the English church, assured everyone that it could be made to sound like an organ (which Phonsie said was a step up from the real organ in the real church, though I wouldn't know as I'd never set foot in that church).

Despite all the old stories about Mrs. Coffey's heavy-handedness, the hall was jam-packed for the service – like I said, it was old home week – and things went pretty much according to local custom. Alice Freeman was brought over from Inverness to sing a couple of Gaelic hymns, though Iain Dubh could have done it.

The Landing, indeed all around this end of Loch Bras d'Or, had been settled by Highland Gaels, and although their language had slipped from use, the underlying culture was overwhelmingly Gaelic. I don't suppose Perk had any of the Gaelic, but you can't live around here without getting a feel for it. She'd have been no different.

Another frequent contributor to funerals was the aforementioned Iain Dubh – still a bachelor scraping by on what his late parents' run-down family farm could provide, along with odd jobs around the village, like Mrs. Coffey's lawn.

Iain Dubh was a dour sort – thus his nickname Black John, Iain Dubh in the Gaelic – and one of the last few native Gaelic speakers in Cape Breton. Native, meaning he was born and raised in the Gaelic. In true Highland fashion, he could be as generous with his wit, time and muscle as he was with a complaint and with his fists.

He was quite the singer, though. He could sometimes be heard quietly singing *puirt-a-beul* as he went about a repetitive or mundane chore, or loudly reciting some song or other alternately praising or skewering some Highland hero or political scoundrel.

∞∞

Iain Dubh was a character alright – every village has one, or more – the sort that people love but don't really respect, and make little jokes about, like that story from the schoolyard long ago. He didn't have a lot going for him. Aside from his marginal subsistence, Iain Dubh's stutter when speaking English, which he had to do almost all of the time after his parents died, cast him as an outsider.

Curiously, he did not stutter in the Gaelic – did I mention that? Only in the English – and he was a bit of a celebrity in that regard. My grandmother once said that was the magic of the Gaelic, but most people figured it was a curse put on him by faeries – or maybe even by Mrs. Coffey. Still, his stutter meant that he didn't get much respect most of his life; people don't have a lot of patience when a conversation takes too long. Adding to his difficulties, everyone figured that Iain Dubh could neither read nor write very well because, like I said, he never finished school.

Iain Dubh's parents and grandparents – Lochaber MacDonalds – were reluctant to send him to the English-only school in the first place. Whether for fear of his losing his mother tongue or for fear of being unable to help him through school; they might have looked stupid in his eyes. There was probably no shortage of disapproval for the secularity of the school either, so they weren't the ones to force him to go back once he quit.

Mrs. Coffey understood the tensions between Protestant and Catholic camps in the villages and the glens and didn't insist on prayers or religious displays in school unless there was a visitor present – which wasn't often. Still, Iain Dubh missed those important years and never learned to read more than necessary to order and fetch supplies. And there was that stutter.

∞∞

Because of his Gaelic it came as no surprise that when it was time for Mrs. Coffey's funeral dirge, it was Iain Dubh who rose from his seat and walked respectfully to the front of the hall for a song or a poem. It was a brief journey, but his ascension was accompanied by whispers and knowing nods. For some tongue-waggers, it was confirmation of his relationship with the deceased.

Iain Dubh had a wonderful repertoire of Gaelic songs, and he broke into one I hadn't heard before – not that I can distinguish many. When he was finished, there were nods of approval, followed by an awkward smattering of applause which exposed the diverse backgrounds of the gathering. People shifted in their seats in anticipation of a change of pace in the program when Iain Dubh should have returned to his seat.

He didn't. He stayed at his spot, shifting his weight a little awkwardly as he reached into his pocket and drew out, first, a pair of spectacles, which no one had ever seen him wear before – and which he put on – then a neatly folded sheet of paper from the pocket of his wrinkled shirt, damp from nervous sweat. This he carefully smoothed out on the lectern in front of him in that way that people have.

It took a moment, but there came a perceptible change in people's focus; they sat more upright at the sight of Iain Dubh with a written speech in front of him. One or two ignorant people snickered, feeling superior in their knowledge that Iain Dubh was going to make for a painfully long speech on account of his stutter.

"'D-dis should be g-go-good," whispered Phonsie, which earned him elbows to his ribs from both sides. The majority, bless them, stayed more or less respectful – though no doubt full of anticipation.

"Th-th-that w-was '*Marbhrann do Mhr Seumas Beattie*,' le Eòghann MacLachlainn," he said, looking out and not down at his paper. "E-elegy on m-Mr. James b-Beattie, by e-e-Ewen MacLachlan. M-MacLachlan was a b-bard from L-Loch-Lochaber. He w-was a t-t-teacher t-too. D-died eighteen-to-wenty-two, a-a-round the t-time many of our p-p-people were c-c-coming here to n-No-Nova Scotia."

I held my breath for him. Others squirmed uncomfortably in their seats. Iain Dubh nervously smoothed his paper again. Squinting down at it in that way that people have, he began to speak, only this time in a surprisingly clear and determined voice.

"There w-wasn't many Gaelic songs or poems dedicated to teachers, especially women. I thought this one would do, because it honours teachers for their values."

"E-e-uphemia C-c-offey," he paused – whether for effect or to be sure he got the next bit right – then looked down at his paper again determinedly.

"Mrs. Coff–" he looked up, winked at us, and added "P-Perk," then returned his attention to his paper. "She were the kind of person in books you read about or see in movies. Yet, here she was, with us, all those years."

Looking up, he reflected, "d-di-did you know s-sh-she wanted t-to be a m-mu-musician? Sh-she- never g-got t-the chance, between t-ta-takin' care o' us an-an her husband." Mention of Mr. Coffey drew a few sad nods among the elders gathered.

From his paper, Iain Dubh continued. "She maybe could have lived and worked almost anywhere, but she stayed here. With us. Taught us things we maybe wouldn't have knowed on our own.

"Who among us hasn't been touched by her in one way or another." Then he snickered, exaggeratedly rubbing his left ear; probably half the men in the room likewise touched an ear in absentminded empathy. There was a murmur of agreement.

"You are probably surprised to see me up here making a speech."

"To say d' lees, son," muttered Phonsie.

"Mrs. Coffey taught me. See, she read somewheres that stutterin' might be self c-consciousness, but if you followed the words on a paper, you might not – might not st-stutter, that is.

"She called me in from her yard one day and explained it to me. I told her it made no difference because I couldn't do that very well either – r-read well, that is."

He looked up to see if we were following.

"S-she j-just s-smiled, a-and waited f-f-for me t-to f-figure that ow-ow-out."

Turning his eyes back to the paper, he continued. "It took a long time," he hesitated – his voice cracking for a moment, and I think almost everyone, whether they knew it or not, felt his emotion – "a long, long time," he repeated distantly. "I couldn't pay her, so I helped around her house. She never gave up. She never let me give up, and she kept my secret.

"It took a long time," he repeated. "We known probably what you was sayin' about us – but she didn't give up.

"And here I am. And here we are. Mrs. Coffey was a fixture in this community, touching everyone in one way or another. That is rare, isn't it?"

Phonsie leaned close to me, miming a slap with the back of his left hand, "touched you a few times too, eh?"

"Like many fixtures in our village, in our lives, she was just kind of— she was just there, always there. Like our parents, our grandparents, our ancestors, like the big trees down by the store. They just always been there.

"And she honoured those things, our things, she really did. Just she wanted to show us there was more. Not that we have less or that some things are better, but we can be better by being aware of them. She was tough. She wanted us to be tough. She never said to turn our backs on our way of life, on our language, or religion, or our friends, but instead to make the most of them."

You could have heard a proverbial pin drop if not for the rhythmic flutter of the hall's ceiling fans. Men standing at the back – having given up their seats to the more elderly – began to show signs of restlessness. This was a side of Iain Dubh that was unfamiliar. For that matter, it was rare to witness any speech-making in these parts without an election in the wind – not even for a fancy funeral.

Iain Dubh looked up as if searching for words. "L-like I s-said. M-mrs. C-coffey l-l-left her m-mark on a-all all u-us. There's lots more folks here l-like me le-le-learned f-f-from her l-l-later on-on their o-o-own. Sh-she n-n-never t-turned any of us a-a-away." He scanned the familiar faces in the congregation, adding, "sh-she kept your s-see-secrets t-too."

Looking down again, he resumed. "Old people die. Teachers, the good ones anyway, live on in us like our parents and grandparents do. Things about them that annoyed us as children eventually bubble up to be passed on yet again.

"Sometimes a teacher is judged by the character of famous and successful students. Nobody famous ever came from the Landing that I know of, though there's plenty of characters. I think Mrs. Coffey was more interested in character than in characters.

"Schools sometimes act like they want to take local character *out* of us, to make us sound alike and think alike."

To myself, I thought, that's how school seemed to me; why else would we need to learn "The Rhyme of the Ancient Mariner"? I thought about Iain Dubh and his Gaelic and how there was hardly anyone speaking it now. I suppose English schooling had a lot to do with that.

"Though she probably had plenty of stories about us," Iain Dubh was reading, "she could of written a book, I never heard her say a unkind word about anyone directly. She wacked me upside the head often enough in school – when I went – but she never said anything mean to me."

He looked up. "S-same f-for y-you, aw-all of us, I-I think – 'cept maybe young Ph-ph-ph-onsie there." He grinned, then looked more serious. "I wr-wrote more than-than I-I s-should of," he said suddenly, glancing down at his paper like he was scanning how much was still there.

"S-she n-never wr-wrote a b-b-book, but but I-I heard her-heard her p-play p-pi-ano. Sh-she was p-pretty good t-too. I'm-I'm pr-pretty sh-sure sh-she n-never wrote any m-mu-music, but...

"Do y-you know wh-what opus me-means? I-it m-means a b-body of mu-mu-music."

Iain Dubh looked down at his paper again. "Mrs. Coffey, she had an opus – us. We are her music. We are like different songs on a record, different chapters in a book. We just don't notice or appreciate it while it's being written, but I reco'nize it now, thanks to Mrs. Coffey."

He paused dramatically, picked up and started to re-fold his paper so we'd know that the service was nearing the end.

"Th-the ch-church l-la-ladies," he stopped for a second, then started again, more slowly. "Ev-everyone is invited downstairs for a reception and light lunch. Maybe share their own s-st-stories about Mrs. Cof— Well, I g-guess she wouldn't mind... Perk."

After a hymn and closing prayer, Phonsie jumped to his feet and grinned. "No more Coffey, time for tea!"

fin

FRESH FISH

"**I** think I'm in love." Lewis MacFarlane stopped mid-sweep as an open-top REO touring car pulled up to the gas pump at MacDonald's store where he was trying to keep up with the dust from morning traffic.

Effie MacDonald good-naturedly elbowed her beefy employee back to his sweeping. "You and cars."

Effie operated MacDonald's General Store. She'd taken over the family business officially two years before when her father died unexpectedly.

Lewis and Effie had been inseparable in childhood. Most people in the village took it for granted that they'd be together forever, but fate had intervened. Her older brother, Ephram, to whom the business would normally have transferred, was also dead.

Ephram had come home from the war wounded inside and out. For years he and his demons lived in an abandoned travel trailer back the mountain, coming to the village for supplies only rarely. Those supplies included ingredients for his homebrew – what passed locally for whisky. After a long absence from public scrutiny, he was found wasted away in his trailer.

The death was hard on both their parents, but especially on their mother. When her husband died she pretty much retreated to her bedroom. Though she had applied to be the store's recognized owner – females needed their husband or father's approval to be in business – she left Effie to take care of everything.

That took away any chance of Effie and Lewis getting together – at least for the foreseeable future. She was too hard at work to cater to a man's need for attention, and he wasn't entirely comfortable with her "wearing the pants," as the old saying goes.

It wasn't resentment per se. Lewis wasn't even sure what he was feeling, but the long-term relationship everyone had taken for granted seemed somehow in doubt, and he occasionally took the opportunity to show it. Like on the day the brand new REO touring car pulled into The Landing's store and filling station.

The weather had been consistently warm and dry, though it was still May. The hardwood trees were barely tinged with green. Dust from traffic up and down the road and around The Landing's numerous wharves and jetties created the only clouds in the mid-day sky.

Automobiles and tourists were nothing new, though it was a bit early in the season, but this was different – rather, the contents of the car were different. When it stopped and the dust settled, and the driver got out, everything on both sides of the road also stopped. It wasn't every day that four women, none of them local, in a brand new open-top REO made a stop in the hamlet. Of course, The Landing was positively cosmopolitan compared with the scattering of steads dotting the hills and shore eastward along Loch Bras d'Or between here and the busy mining town of Marble Mountain.

"It's not polite to stare," Effie said stiffly out of the corner of her mouth. Lewis had made no secret of his interest in the unfolding scene but, trying to remain nonchalant, Effie turned her attention back to inspecting the bags of feed Lewis had a short time ago stacked to await pick up from the front corner of the veranda.

No doubt Lewis's attention was divided between curiosity about the passengers and admiration for their automobile. Out of the corner of her eye, Effie saw the car door open and the driver emerge tall and straight.

"Afternoon ladies." Without having to look around, Effie could picture Lewis gallantly touching his tweed cap in deference.

"You'll have to forgive my friend here," said Effie. She self-consciously raised her hand to tuck a few loose strands of hair back beneath her kertch. "We don't get many tourists, and he's lacking in manners."

That was true so far as Lewis's manners, but not about local traffic. There was a fair bit to and through The Landing. Two tanneries, the carriage maker across the road, the sawmill, a tailor, several stores and around seventy active farms between here and Marble Mountain made for quite a lot of traffic, actually. But it was still mostly horse-drawn – not to mention the commercial traffic to the limestone quarry there and the water-borne traffic on the loch.

But four women travelling unaccompanied in an expensive open car was definitely a rarity. As the three passengers stood and stretched, the rarity became even more pronounced. Effie supposed they ranged in age from early twenties to mid-forties; they were dressed in the fashions of the times, though rather manly, in her opinion.

The middle-aged driver was wearing a loose-fitting wool shirt only partially tucked into the waistband of her full-knickerbockers. On her head, a light-coloured wide-brimmed felt hat was secured by a plain broad sash that doubled as a hat band. Two of the others sported similar headgear, one in place and one hanging down her back by a leather thong. That hat had a large eagle feather sticking out of its band. The youngest woman – Effie figured her to be about her age, twenty-something – wore a fashionable straw hat.

"Why, hello Katherine!" Effie was startled from her reverie by a raspy male voice behind her. "What brings you to The Landing?"

Murdoch MacPhie crossed the veranda, went down the steps and inserted himself into the scene. Effie took an involuntary step backward – a move she instantly regretted.

She sometimes found it exhausting to be a woman in business, and she constantly felt that she had to work harder to gain equal footing with older and more established businessmen like MacPhie. He ran several enterprises, many of which had been in his family for nearly a century – including the Carriage House Inn right in the village. On top of that, he was the largest landowner, something which made most people regard him warily. He was never hostile or openly disdainful of Effie – so far as she could tell – yet she was instinctively intimidated by him.

"Hello Mr. MacPhie. Murdoch, right?" The lady driver stepped toward him and extended her hand in greeting. Effie sensed that MacPhie recoiled for an instant at the woman's forwardness, but he recovered quickly and took her hand as she greeted him.

"How nice to see you, Murdoch. My friends and I are on a little road trip. They've not been up this way before, and it's been such a long time since father and I were here. It's truly lovely, isn't it?"

"And how is your father?" asked MacPhie.

"He is quite well, thank you for asking. Very busy of course. I spent much of the winter with him in Ottawa.

He returned to Petersfield just a few weeks ago. It seems his second home now, rather than his main residence."

"Do I understand that you have taken up his cause at Louisburg?"

"Why yes, how kind of you to know that. It has become a passion of mine as well."

Effie felt she should be part of this conversation, taking place as it was at her front door, so to speak.

"How can we help you today, Mrs—?"

"McLennan, Katharine," the driver said, giving Effie her attention and extending a hand in greeting. She introduced the bareheaded woman as Frances Setchell, the eagle-feathered as Clara Burchell and the youngest as Ella Liscombe.

MacPhie jumped in, "of the mining Burchells, perhaps? I probably know your father, I should think.

Turning officiously back to Effie, he puffed, "Miss McLennan's – Katharine's – father is J. S. McLennan. Senator J. S. McLennan." Effie thought he overemphasized 'Senator' unnecessarily.

"My friends and I plan to stay at Grand Anse for a few days," said Katharine. "Take in some of the scenery—"

"Katharine is quite the artist," interrupted MacPhie, again addressing Effie. "She takes after her mother, whose paintings hang in some important galleries in Montreal and Ottawa. Isn't that right, Katharine?" He didn't seem too concerned that her party would be staying at MacPherson's hotel rather than his own.

"My friends are much more talented than I." Katharine turned toward her fellow travellers, "Ella here is also a bit of a poet, we are learning." The young woman, Ella, was busy photographing the scene across the road with a Brownie camera; a minor commotion announced a brand new carriage being carefully wheeled out of its factory by a half-dozen workers.

Murdoch MacPhie excused himself and started across the road to inspect his factory's latest edition, calling over his shoulder, "let me know if you need anything while you are in the area Katharine. Just ask anyone for me. And please tell the Senator I asked after him."

"I shall Murdoch, thank you." Turning quickly back to Effie, she said, "the weather is grand. We'll likely spend quite a bit of time out-of-doors and will need some additional supplies for a picnic in addition to the petrol, I should think." Lewis, standing next to the car, retrieved the hose from the petrol pump.

"I wonder if you can give me some directions – Effie, is it? We wish to visit at Ballam Head on our way to Black River. A Mr. Andrews. Do you know it?"

"Yes, of course. It's about three miles toward Dundee. Do you know Mr. Andrews?"

"Not personally, no. Yet. But I have, of course, heard of the famous tapestries – stitched by his blind aunts, I believe? The Ballam sisters? I was hoping to discuss them with him."

"You may be too late. People say he sold them."

"I heard that too – a shame. Such treasures should remain in Cape Breton...." She paused. "Nonetheless, we shall seek him out, as it is not out of our way."

Having finished refuelling the REO, Lewis stepped back onto the veranda. "All set. Did I hear something about Dundee?"

Katherine half-turned. "Yes. Yes, we shall call there on the way to our lodgings. I recall a lovely spot for picnics and painting near the river."

"Really." Up beside Effie now, Lewis looked at the REO and the other women surveying the activity at the carriage factory and the scenic cove beyond. "I suppose you'll do a little fishing while you're there."

Effie recognized the smirk in his tone and gave him a look meant to put him in his place, but it was Katherine who spoke. "That's a good idea, young man." Then, with a twinkle in her eye she said to Effie, "perhaps you have fishing poles, or at least line and hooks? We could craft our own poles if need be. We would normally camp out, but it's a bit early in the year."

She took a step toward the door of the store, deferring briefly so Effie could lead the way. "Let us see what else we shall need."

The four of them – Effie, Katharine and two of her companions – headed into the store, leaving Lewis to turn his attention to the young photographer. "That's a fine looking camera you have there," he said, descending to the road.

As they watched, activity on the wharf and the road returned to normal and they and the REO were absorbed by the dust-and-pollen-covered streetscape, while others shopped inside.

∞∞

"Maybe I should look in on the lady tourists," Lewis said casually to Effie the next morning. "See if they need anything."

"That would be very gallant of you." Her back turned, Effie rolled her eyes in that way that women do.

"Just trying to be hospitable," Lewis grinned as he took off his apron. "My chores finished—" He hesitated, "right?"

"Right."

Effie was getting used to the dynamics of their changing relationship over the last while. It is rare for a woman to run a business, a young woman at least.

There were a number of older women, widows mainly, who ran farms or took in sewing and washing, but it was generally expected that young women were to marry, or go into female pursuits – teacher, nun, nurse.

Lewis probably had the same expectations where he and Effie were concerned, but their relationship had been strained by Effie's responsibilities. He had gone away for awhile to work on a farm on the mainland – implausible given he had failed to distinguish himself as a farmer, or even as a farm hand, on a farm just down the road.

Then he thought he might get work in one of the coal mines down in Glace Bay or New Waterford, but a prolonged – and sometimes violent – strike had spoiled that prospect. While he marked time and contemplated his future, Effie offered him a job at the store. She had to offer more than once because his male pride bade him decline, but now he was working steady. His income helped out his parents a bit, and he was saving money to buy a car. Hopefully. If things didn't improve around here, he could drive his car westward until he found something else.

Removing his apron as he went, Lewis walked through the store and into the backroom where he exchanged it for his jacket. His cap was always already on his head.

"See you day after tomorrow," he yelled over his shoulder. "Maybe I'll bring you a fresh fish for your supper."

An hour later, Lewis stopped in at his parents' house at Rear Black River, grabbed his fishing pole and his rifle, and set out on the familiar path toward Dundee.

∞∞

Katharine and her two older friends had set up their easels in a loch-side clearing where the Black River delivers its iron-rich waters beneath the new iron bridge. The girl, Ella, had set her Brownie camera on a stand at the edge of the clearing and was focusing her attention on the larger scene: their picnic site, the women artists, and the loch and mountains beyond. It was a clear afternoon with not so much humidity as to be hazy. Absorbed by their creative endeavours, the four were oblivious to being watched.

The scene, as Ella obviously could interpret, was right out of a painting. And from Lewis's vantage point, he could see what she saw – the women and their easels, their khaki outfits almost blending into the not-yet fully green late spring. A sizeable army-issue tent was set up for shade rather than for camping, he guessed, since the women had implied they would be staying at MacPherson's Hotel.

A thin column of smoke rose from a modest campfire, next to which a large iron pot sat on a makeshift stand. On a nearby patch of grass sat a large wicker picnic hamper. From his vantage, Lewis could just make out its contents – plates, glasses and perhaps checkered napkins. He could see a bundle, probably provisions, suspended in a nearby tree, a precaution wisely taken to deter wildlife from sharing the contents. The car was nowhere to be seen but probably just out of sight.

They did not see him, obviously, but more importantly, they did not see the whole picture as he could. They could not see the large black bear at the edge of the forest behind them. Whatever the women planned for lunch must have been of interest to the bear. It was downwind from them, so they didn't smell it. Lewis was downwind from the bear, so it didn't smell him.

Seized by both the potential of harm to the unsuspecting visitors and by generations of Highland chivalry, Lewis checked his gun, and as quickly as he thought practical and safe, he began to descend in a trajectory that would land him between the women and the bear.

That he had not yet considered how to take charge of the situation without startling either the women or the bear – either intervention might prove disastrous – became moot when Lewis tripped over the exposed roots of a tree at the edge of the riverbank, and fell head-over-heels into space. The deafening roar of his rifle discharging in too-close proximity to his ear overcame his senses, and everything was nothing.

∞∞

Lewis became faintly aware of light flickering on the inside of his eyelids inexplicably in concert with a dull roar in his ears and a throbbing in his head. The impulse to sit up was quickly replaced by the need to lie back down, from which position he decided it would be best to calmly survey the situation. He was lying on tree-shaded grass not far from the campfire he had spied from his earlier vantage point. With a start, he remembered what had brought him here.

Manoeuvering onto his left side, Lewis was able to raise himself on his left elbow. As he did, his right arm spontaneously and painfully swung to the front, where it hung suspended by a neatly cinched sling that all but immobilized it. Suffice to say this restricted him somewhat, but his position afforded him an extra few seconds to process things.

"You gave us bit of a scare," said a disembodied female voice. Lewis was facing into the afternoon sun, and being unable to shield his eyes from it, he couldn't make out who was speaking or from where.

By pushing himself to be almost sitting, he was able to turn more toward the voice to see the young girl – 'Ella' he thought – peering over her camera still pointed toward her companions. From his half-prone position near loch level, Lewis could not see the others.

"And the bear?" he asked.

"Bear?!" Ella turned her head this way and that so quickly that Lewis thought she might twist something.

"Long gone no doubt," he said, sitting up straighter still. His left arm now free from holding him up, Lewis habitually motioned to adjust his cap, but instead of its reassuring tweed firmness, he discovered his head was bandaged.

"Does it hurt much?" Ella mothered.

"I'm not sure, to be honest. What happened?"

"We heard a shout and a shot. We didn't know what had happened. Katherine wanted to investigate. We couldn't talk her out of it."

"How did I get here?"

"We insisted on going with her, and we found you on the beach." She pointed. "Over there. Katherine made a stretcher out of driftwood. We car—"

"You carried me?" The throbbing was becoming more pronounced. Whether it was his body waking to the injuries, or his realization that these women – one of them just a girl – had picked him up, trundled him to their campsite, patched him up, then resumed their little outing, he felt very vulnerable. Not a good feeling for a young man.

He reached up to assess the bandage on his head again but was stopped by a sharp pain in his shoulder.

"Isn't she wonderful? Katharine, I mean. She treated you from her first aid bag in the car. She was a nurse in the war. She's seen much worse – worse than you, I mean – your injuries, I mean – in the war, I mean. You look rather pale—"

"Lewis."

"Ella."

"Where are the others, Ella?"

"Over there on that point. Katharine thought the fishing might be good there too."

"It depends on the tide, but ... she's right."

"This is such a lovely place. A true treasure. Oh, here they come." Without taking her eyes off the scenery, she started to disconnect her Brownie from its stand.

Now sitting, determined to catch his breath and his wits, Lewis looked toward the point, shading his eyes with his free hand. "I best be going," he said, though he didn't try getting to his feet just yet.

"I am certain that Katharine will want to speak with you," said Ella quickly. "You should rest at least until she looks you over."

"I'm fine, really."

"No, you are not fine. I insist. K will insist. We call her K sometimes."

Lewis was torn. His pride was prodding him to shake off his injuries and get going. At the same time, the injuries and his curiosity bade him remain.

Katharine was the first to appear, her stride belying the fact that she had under one arm a large easel and, in that hand, a medium-size canvas held awkwardly away from her loose-fitting knickers. Under her other arm were balanced a box of paints and a pallet. From that hand dangled a short gad from which two fair-sized trout glistened in the sunlight.

Beside her strode a tall man, his reddish blond hair springing out from under a tweed tam. He wore a loose-fitting wool shirt and wool trousers, much too heavy for such a warm day. Lewis recognized him as Hugh MacInnis – Hughie – whose large Victorian home loomed over the new bridge like a tollhouse. MacInnis carried a fishing pole and a single trout.

Behind them, the other two women came into view, each similarly laden, except for the fish. One struggled with three obviously homemade fishing poles, in addition to her paints, her arm hooked through the handles of another wicker basket. Both women were noticeably more winded than their leader.

"Well, it looks like our patient will live, Mr. MacInnis," Katherine announced. "How are you feeling, Mr....?"

"MacFarlane. Lewis. I'm fine. Thanks to you, I'm told."

"You had a nasty fall, Lewis. You were lucky someone was nearby to investigate. When we heard the yell and the shot—"

"My rifle!"

Setting down her various burdens as she spoke, Katherine replied, "secured in the car, along with your fishing rod. What were you shooting at?"

"The bear. No. I think the gun went off when I tripped." He was hearing himself through a dull but persistent roaring in his head.

"Bear?"

"He saw a bear," Ella interjected.

"I wanted to warn you," Lewis said weakly.

"You certainly went to great pains to do that – and to frighten it away," said Katherine. Her sarcasm was not mean-spirited, but Lewis winced defensively in front of MacInnis.

"I should be going," Lewis asserted.

"You lost some blood. You're in no condition to walk any distance just yet. We can drive you. But later. You'll rest a bit longer." It was not a suggestion but an instruction.

She motioned toward the fish. "Join us while these are fresh. I think there is enough to share, unless you th—" In a change of tone, she said, "By then maybe you will be ready to return."

Hughie MacInnis bid them good day, and the four women busied themselves marshalling together their meal – Lewis could not remember the names of the two older women. They appeared to have well-defined tasks as they moved about the camp. Katharine set the fish on a large flat stone and proceeded to gut and fillet them – quickly and expertly, Lewis noted.

One of the older women worked on the fire, positioning a collapsible iron grate over the flames. The other women lowered their supplies from the tree he'd noticed earlier. Ella hurriedly gathered dried sticks of wood from the area around the campsite and a few from the river's edge. She looked nervously over her shoulder and up and down the estuary as she worked.

It wasn't long before the fish were sizzling in an iron skillet over the fire. Heavy porcelain plates with Chinese country scenes in blue, cutlery of silver and goblets of pewter comprised an elegant scene more suited to a senator's estate than any fishing trips Lewis had experienced. Having only four sets, Katharine and the older of the other women shared a plate. He did his best to appear nonchalant, but didn't engage much in the conversation, uncharacteristically opting to speak only when spoken to. The fish was delicious.

For more than an hour, Katharine quizzed him on where he lived, about his neighbours and the Ballams. Pointing across the Black River southeast to the highlands now in the full golden sun of afternoon, asking, "Do you happen to know whose property that is? I know Mr. MacInnis's, of course, but what about beyond? What a lovely view it must be from up there."

Locals don't often consider 'the view,' save for what it affords in reconnaissance for hunting. He knew that outsiders got excited about the scenery for its own sake, but if you couldn't eat from it, drink from it, burn it, or distill it, most locals took it for granted.

His grandparents – refugees from the Highlands of Scotland – hadn't taken it for granted, but Lewis's post-war generation had started looking westward to the rapid industrialization in Upper Canada and the Boston States for comparison. His family was comfortably scraping by in their inherited acreage, but Lewis felt that wasn't enough for him.

"MacRae. Donald Duncan. Owns almost everything from the river here to Cameron Mountain Road. Getting a bit run down, my pa says. No sons to take over. Killed in the war, they were."

"How sad."

"This whole area, this end of the loch used to be farms," Lewis informed her. "They used to refer to West Bay as 'The Garden'."

"Shame. Well, maybe one day people will rediscover it."

Lewis suddenly felt a bit weak and sat down on the boulder next to the fire. The ringing in his ears had been replaced by a faint hum, which seemed to be getting steadily louder. As he struggled to remain composed, he observed Katharine and her companions looking to the skies, hands shading their eyes from the afternoon sun.

The hum got louder and louder, but deeper and more mechanical. Instinctively, Lewis also looked to the sky, just as a single-engine airplane came into view from the southwest, seemingly just above the trees where the river widened. Airplanes were not a common sight over Cape Breton – not uncommon, mind you, just not common. They always gave people pause.

Hughie MacInnis must have found it either strange or exciting. They could see him at the river down from his house, waving his cap excitedly. The airplane droned impassively overhead and into the northeastern skies over the loch; everyone watched until they could no longer distinguish it.

∞∞

The distraction having passed, Katharine suggested it might be good to get going. She walked upstream a few dozen paces and turned off into the trees. Unseen, the REO roared to life, and she skillfully reversed it to be closer to the campsite. Turning off the engine and getting out, she reached into the rear seat and raised it to reveal a dusty storage compartment.

"Here are your rifle and fishing rod."

Lewis, with Ella at his elbow, was pleased and also surprised. Next to his rifle and dismantled fishing rod lay a set of golfing sticks arrayed in a long leather-and-canvas carry bag.

Ella sensed his interest. "K is quite the golfer too." There was a special reverence in her tone, but he couldn't quite place it.

With his good arm, he hefted the rifle like it might be tainted by association with the woman's golfing sticks. Lewis looked it over for signs of damage.

"Golf, eh?" he said distractedly. "Kind of a rich man's game, isn't it?"

"Don't be so old-fashioned," Ella admonished playfully. "Women golf too, don't they K."

Lewis quickly enjoined, "I don't doubt that. It's just that – well, around here, folks are too busy working..." he pointed his precious Springfield rifle into the distance, sighting along the barrel to reassure himself it remained true. Only then did he notice that the bolt action had been removed. He looked to Katharine quizzically.

"I thought it would be a little safer," she said, going to the luggage trunk at the rear of the car.

Unclasping the catches, she reached into the trunk and retrieved the bolt, the spent bullet casing and his cap.

"Can't be too careful," she added. Lewis winced again. His eyes fell once more on the golf sticks.

"Actually," Katharine noted, "golf is a bit like hunting, don't you think?"

Lewis cocked his head to look at her.

"You take target practice whenever you can, walk for hours chasing your quarry, aim carefully, make your shot. If you are a little off, sometimes you have to look for it. Though with golf, nothing gets hurt. Except your pride sometimes. It can be a frustrating game."

Lewis stared at her blankly, searching his mind for a comeback that just wouldn't come. He was saved when Katharine snickered.

"Oh, Lewis, don't look so serious. I'm teasing you. Golf isn't for everyone, but it is a challenge, and it gets you out for fresh air and exercise with a lot of socializing in good measure.

"It's growing in popularity," she continued, "who knows, maybe one day there will be a golf course right here – people might come from far and wide to share your beautiful bay."

"Oh, aye. Maybe old Donald Duncan will take it up and start playing right over there. There could be a big resort – swimming pools, tennis…"

"Now who is teasing whom? But who knows? You must be feeling better. I'll give you a lift if it's not too far – I'd rather be back at MacPherson's for the evening meal."

"I'm fine, but a ride in that car would be finer. It's only a couple of miles."

"I'll return without delay, ladies. We'll have tea by the fire before returning to the inn."

"I could leave you my rifle if you like," offered Lewis. "I could show you how to use it."

"I am quite familiar," Katharine said firmly. "And I would rather not have it here any longer." Her tone changed when she added good-naturedly. "Besides, I doubt that bear has stopped running yet!"

∞∞

Lewis was off the next day but went in to work as usual the day after that. He arrived as scheduled, around the time the mid-morning sun replaced the dampness of night with the dust of traffic. Though still favouring his sore arm and shoulder, out of pride he had dispensed with the sling. His tweed cap once again replaced yesterday's head bandage.

"*Maduinn mhath*, boss," he hollered across to the counter where Effie – back turned – was noisily arranging canisters on a high shelf. He continued to the back room, where he donned his work apron.

"*Maduinn mhath*. Morning," Effie hollered back loud enough for him to hear.

"I'll put away those crates from this morning's deliveries," Lewis offered loudly. He began to first drag and then lift crates of produce.

As he worked, Effie quietly came up close behind him.

"Are you sure you're up to it?" she asked loudly.

Startled, Lewis replied quickly and defensively, "why wouldn't I be?"

"No reason," Effie smiled playfully and half-turned to return to the outer store. Then, turning back to face him, she added, "oh, how was the fishing? I thought you might bring some with you this morning."

"Fine, fine. Ate them for supper. Sorry."

"By the way, Miss McLennan was in early this morning on her way to Baddeck."

Lewis felt himself blush.

"She said to say hello. You must have made quite an impression; she asked how you were feeling."

"Oh yeah? Well..."

"She seems quite the accomplished woman."

"I guess."

"Driving, camping, fishing. An artist too. She doesn't seem to rely too much on anyone for anything."

"She was a nurse in the war," Lewis added.

"Oh, that's what she meant when she said she had patched up her share of young men who had mishaps with guns."

Effie could no longer keep a straight face and quickly changed the subject. "Katharine said you all had a brush with history."

Lewis was puzzled.

"The telegraph office at MacPherson's said that the airplane you saw was on its way to Europe, a Mr. Lindbergh, I think she said. Can you imagine? Well, we best be getting back to it. I have a business to run."

"Yes you do." Lewis bent back to his work. But he stopped and called out, "and it's a good business, thanks to you. Even better than before." Turning back to his work, he didn't wait for a reply.

Effie stopped and turned to look at him thoughtfully.

"It's not easy," she said. "I know it's not easy between us – not easy for you. So, thank you."

Lewis flushed and, in that way that men have, he deflected her gesture. "Well, it's not like you play golf or anything."

Effie let out a laugh and turned once more to leave. "Golf?" she questioned. "Who has time for golf? Especially a woman. That's a rich man's sport."

Lewis shrugged, then, like it was something he said every day, "want to go fishing after church Sunday? I know a good spot for a picnic."

fin

A WET COAST TALE

I dreamed it would end like this – at the bar, solitary, besotted, trousers soaking wet, a puddle of my own making edging slowly toward the snooker table where a bunch of locals were intent on their match.

They were oblivious to the tentacle of liquid creeping toward the feet of the bigger of the lot as he struggled to focus on his next shot. Should he discover the puddle, and me as its source, things might not end well. Deep inside me, a cord unwinds, like a dishcloth having discharged its liquid burden.

In my dream I'm old, confused, incontinent. In reality, I'm at the bar in Ben Arthur's Bothy, as dripping wet as I've ever been, having just spent the day in the Alps – not those Alps, the other ones, the Alps of Arrochar, in the west of Scotland – where I'd had a date with Beinn Artair, The Cobbler, who, just so you know, didn't show.

Nine hours ago, I got off the coach at Tarbet – not Tarbert; not the one on Harris either; Tarbet, on Loch Lomond. I'd caught the wrong coach from Glasgow, and had to walk the extra miles to Arrochar, the coach driver's derision ringing in my ears. The fog and the rain suited my self-recrimination for the error.

In a loch-side park in Arrochar, I was mocked by a decaying chainsaw carving of a Viking that, to be honest, looked a lot like a squatting monkey. That image had lifted my spirits a little. The real healing began as I stepped off the local forest park trail through a curtain of mist and rain waving down the strath onto the gravel path lined by brown and lifeless bracken.

At the mid-point of the walk stands a pair of sentinels, two of hundreds of erratics left behind by the ice-age equivalent of a tsunami or perhaps hived off the formidable cliffs to the north, evidence of some leviathan struggle. The cliffs weep, like many in the Highlands, as though they, and they alone, are responsible for keeping the loch and the oceans full.

It is difficult to convey the deep sense of self that one finds in the Highlands, wet and miserable though they can be. I sometimes feel as though I was born with the express purpose of being there.

As I leaned into the modest grade, an idiotic grin stretched my face – my inner cord winding up in excitement, a store of energy to be called upon at some future moment.

At the end of the footpath, at the feet of The Cobbler, irony mixed with the rainwater that filled my boots. Like me, he had his head in the clouds, and we failed to meet as promised.

Strange to be simultaneously soaking wet and thirsty, unless your hydration ritual includes lager, as mine does. Beinn Artair, the Cobbler, disappointed but Ben Arthur's bothy provided the required refuge.

Having discharged its burden of liquid sunshine, the inner cord unwound slowly, the release cathartic. The coach back to reality, to Glasgow, is nigh.

fin

NOTES AND INSPIRATIONS

Thanks to Gail Jones for her assist. Thanks to Carol Corbin for her insights, especially on "Still Life" (p. 52).

"Maddie's Gifts" (p. 1). "1950 Blue" comes from a great Ian Tyson (1933-2022) song, "Casey Tibbs" (*I Outgre The Wagon*, Universal Music Canada). I love the descriptive line: "The sky was 1950 blue."

A fascinating postcript regarding 'Maddie's telephone' can be found in a CBC article filed years after the story was originally written. Here's a TinyURL to the story: https://tinyurl.com/4as7cvsk .

"The New Girl" (p. 10). An early version of this story was accepted by *The Nashwaak Review* vol. 42, but it appears the publication has folded; just my luck.

"Mac Talla – The Echo" (p. 20). 'Mi'kmaw' is the adjectival use of 'Mi'kmaq'. Thanks to piper Barry Shears for some advice on this story. An early version was written for a competition. That version failed muster but I didn't want to give up on the ideas spawned, and kept working on it.

"Poor Woolly and the Bear" (p. 33). This story was initially composed to enter a competition on the theme of the circus. The character Poor Woolly is partly inspired by an observation of a young man in a large bookstore in Toronto. We have all seen such individuals, but I was struck by his engagement with the book he was reading. While standing, his periodic surveillance of the people around him seemed as though he was relating them to what he was reading. He gently and rhythmically swayed back and forth as he read, perhaps to a tune in his head. An acquaintance, now deceased, from North Sydney, Nova Scotia, David Wilkie was always around the racetrack (Standardbreds) in North Sydney. He was quite brilliant but very intense. His personality we today would characterize as somewhere on the autism spectrum. Another Poor Woolly story is included in *No PLace Like Home*

"Dick and Jane (and Barbie)" (p. 44) was short-listed for the Tarbert Book Festival Flash-Fiction Competition, 2017.

"Jack and Jill" (p. 49) was long-listed for the Tarbert Book Festival Flash-Fiction Competition, 2018.

"Still Life" (p. 52). Thanks to Carol Corbin for her patient insights and help rethinking this story. Duckie gets his name from the Duckbill Loader, an underground coal loading machine. I imagine its early 1950s incorporation into local mines as introduced by 'Franklin (Duckie) Dennis.' There is a kernel of truth to the genesis of this story. *Have Gun, Will Travel* was a hit TV series following the adventures of a man calling himself "Paladin" (played by Richard Boone). Paladin is a gentleman investigator/gunfighter who travels around the Old West working as a mercenary for people who hire him to solve their problems, usually with gunfire.

"Mrs. Coffey's Opus" (p. 77). Irene MacDonald, West Bay Road, grew up in Marble Mountain. She once made reference to someone who was the first person in that village to have a television. Iain Dubh and his stutter are inspired by a story of a Gaelic speaker from River Denys, NS. That man apparently stuttered in English but not in the Gaelic. He was once described to me by Barbara MacKay, West Bay. While Coffey is a settler name found in property records around St. George's Channel, Mrs. Coffey (a.k.a. Perk) was also the name of a long-time kindergarten teacher in Riverview, NB. I still remember some of her lessons.

"Fresh Fish" (p. 96) references and combines a number of historical incidents and characters. They are all used fictitiously, of course, but there are kernels of truth.

Katharine McLennan (1892-1975) was a prominent Cape Breton figure known for her advocacy of the town of Louisbourg's history, a history researched and published by her father, Senator J.S. McLennan. Their research and her perseverance are credited with the marvellous historical reconstruction that is The Fortress of Louisbourg National Historic Site of Canada. Katharine served as a nurse in field hospitals during the First World War and was an accomplished artist.

Many facts about Katharine's life have gotten little attention over the years, save for the efforts of the McConnell Memorial Library (Sydney, NS), which she founded, and Parks Canada historian (ret.) A.J.B. Johnston (who in recent years self-published a book with Katharine at the centre, *Something True*, 2018). There resides in the Beaton Institute at Cape Breton University, a small photo album donated by the Liscombe family that recounts a road trip made by Katharine and a few friends (whose names are re-counted in this story), including young Ella Liscombe who was apparently responsible for the photographs and accompanying poetry in the album. It should be noted, however, that the road trip it recounts (Ingonish and environs) conflicts over dates with an unpublished typescript of McLennan's memoirs held in the McConnell Library collections.

De Gary Andrews was a descendant of the Ballams and a resident of Ballam Head, Dundee; the tapestries created by his aunts are historical artifacts of lost provenance.

On May 20, 1927, at 3:15 p.m., Charles Lindberg flew *Spirit of St. Louis* directly over Dundee and Bras d'Or Lake on his historic solo transatlantic flight from New York to Paris. Details of the flight suggest an altitude of between 300 and 600 ft. It was witnessed by Mr. Hughie MacInnis, who lived in the first home on the right when you cross the bridge over Black River heading south.

In the 1970s, the Cape Breton Development Corporation (Devco) acquired land previously owned, at least in part, by Donald Douglas MacRae; Dundee Golf Club (and resort) was thereon constructed (source: Ross Wagg, St. Georges Channel, 2019). I thought Katharine McLennan's close ties to Devco (re: Louisbourg) and her interest in golf, would make a fun forerunner of the resort at Dundee.

The MacPherson House/Hotel in Grand Anse began life as a stagecoach stop; it was also, at various times, the telegraph house and the post office. It became a hotel in 1923 and ceased business in 1969.

"A Wet Coast Tale" (p. 116) was short-listed for the Tarbert Book Festival Flash-Fiction Competition, 2016, on the general theme of the west coast (of Scotland). It stems from a hike I once made to The Cobbler in the Arrochar "Alps," Argyll, Scotland.

M IKE R. HUNTER is former Editor-in-Chief at
Cape Breton University Press (retired). He has
an MA in Communication and Culture from York and
Ryerson (now Toronto Metropolitan) universities.

A native of Riverview, NB, Mike has lived all over
Canada, and in Cape Breton since 1984. He's been as-
sociated with the university since 1996. He took over
the press in 2003, guiding it from publishing four books
annually to ten books annually by 2016.

Related experiences include managing editor of
a small-town newspaper, freelance for the Halifax
Chronicle Herald and other periodicals, as well as publication of a few articles in academic presses.

Some flash fiction stories have been long- and
shortlisted for various prizes. The good folks at Tarbert
Book Festival, Scotland, have shortlisted two flash fiction pieces. The original story "A Wing and a Prayer"
won Ed's Books short fiction competition (Sydney,
NS, 2018) and was subsequently published in the *Cape
Breton Post*. Many other submissions have so far failed
to make the grade – too bad for them – making this
self-publication necessary (he needed to get these stories off his desk in order to move on).

A previous collection, *No Place Like Home: Short
Stories from the Landing*, was self-published in the fall,
2022, with Kindle Direct Publishing (KDP).

Mike and families live in West Bay, Cape Breton,
and Toronto. He edits non-fiction books for others, and
is working on a novel of his own. When not hunched
over a manuscript, he may be found on the trails – hik-
ing in summer, snowshoeing in winter – or having
coffee and telling stories with the locals.